STUCK ON THE U. S. A.

Fascinating Facts About the 50 States!

P9-CLC-767

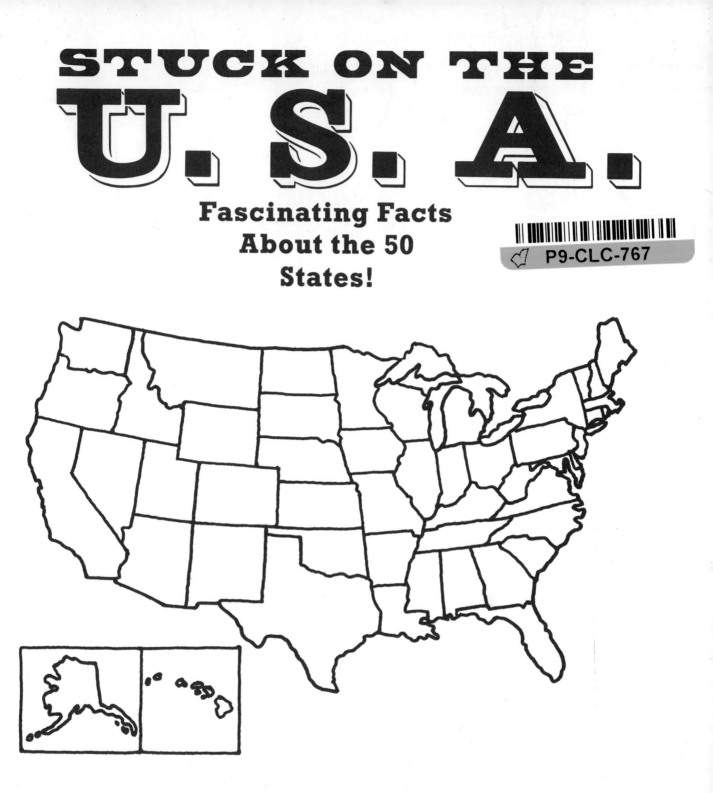

Cover illustration by Gus Alavezos
Sticker art by Paul Harvey, Edward Heins, and Kathie Kelleher
Line art by Ron Fritz

Text copyright © 1994 by Grosset & Dunlap, Inc., a member of The Putnam & Grosset Group, New York.
Cover illustration copyright © 1994 by Gus Alavezos. Sticker art copyright © 1994 by Paul Harvey,
Edward Heins, and Kathie Kelleher. Line art copyright © 1994 by Ron Fritz. All rights reserved.
Published by Grosset & Dunlap, Inc., a member of The Putnam & Grosset Group, New York.
GROSSET & DUNLAP is a trademark of Grosset & Dunlap, Inc. Published simultaneously in Canada.
Printed in the U.S.A. Library of Congress Catalog Card Number: 93-78597 ISBN 0-448-40179-7
C D E F G H I J

WASHINGTON

MONTANA

NORTH DAKOTA

OREGON

IDAHO

SOUTH DAKOTA

WYOMING

NEBRASKA

NEVADA

UTAH

COLORADO

CALIFORNIA

KANSAS

ARIZONA

NEW MEXICO

OKLAHOM

PACIFIC OCEAN

TEXAS

ALASKA

HAWAII

MEXICO

2

CANADA

MAINE

VT.

N.H.

MASS.

MINNESOTA

WISCONSIN

MICHIGAN

NEW YORK

CONN.

R.I.

IOWA

PENNSYLVANIA

N.J.

OHIO

MD.

DEL.

INDIANA

Washington, D.C.

ILLINOIS

WEST VIRGINIA

The city marked by a star isn't in any state. It's the capital of the U.S.A.— Washington, D.C.!

MISSOURI

VIRGINIA

KENTUCKY

NORTH CAROLINA

TENNESSEE

SOUTH CAROLINA

ARKANSAS

GEORGIA

ATLANTIC OCEAN

MISSISSIPPI

ALABAMA

LOUISIANA

FLORIDA

GULF OF MEXICO

N

W   E

S

What does U.S.A. stand for? **UNITED STATES OF AMERICA!**
Fifty states are united under one government to make up the U.S.A.

3

ALABAMA
THE YELLOWHAMMER STATE

Alabama's capital, Montgomery, also served as a capital of the Confederacy during the Civil War, making Alabama the true "Heart of Dixie."

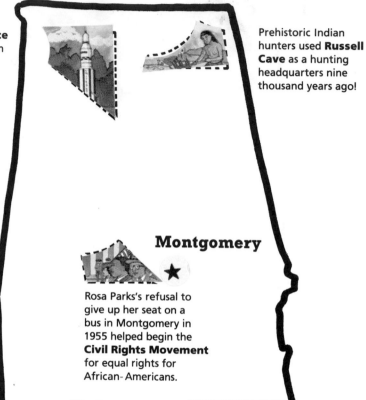

At the **Alabama Space and Rocket Center** in Huntsville, visitors can fire laser beams and pilot simulated spacecraft to the surface of the moon!

Prehistoric Indian hunters used **Russell Cave** as a hunting headquarters nine thousand years ago!

Montgomery

★

Rosa Parks's refusal to give up her seat on a bus in Montgomery in 1955 helped begin the **Civil Rights Movement** for equal rights for African-Americans.

Alabama's nickname dates back to the Civil War, when the state's troops wore uniforms trimmed in bright yellow. They reminded people of a bird called the yellowhammer, which has yellow patches under its wing.

State Flag

Camellia

Yellowhammer

License Plate

Helen Keller heroically overcame blindness and deafness to become a great educator of the 1900s. Born in Alabama in 1880, she is a symbol of courage and hope.

Find the ALABAMA stickers on sticker page A.

ALASKA
THE LAST FRONTIER

Alaska is so big that if you set it down in the continental U.S.A., it would stretch all the way from California to Florida!

The **Trans-Alaska Pipeline** carries oil from Prudhoe Bay to the port of Valdez—almost eight hundred miles!

Each year, mushers and their dog teams race across Alaska in the 1,049-mile **Iditarod Sled Dog Race**. The trip can take anywhere from ten to twenty days!

At 20,320 feet, **Mount McKinley** is the tallest mountain in North America. Each year, hundreds of expert climbers make it to the top.

Juneau

Because Alaska is so close to the North Pole, it's almost always dark in the winter. During the summer, the sun shines almost twenty-four hours a day. It's called the "midnight sun."

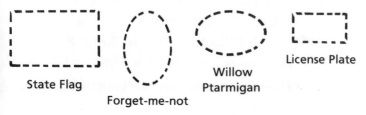

State Flag

Forget-me-not

Willow Ptarmigan

License Plate

Find the ALASKA stickers on sticker page A.

In the winter of 1925, a diphtheria epidemic threatened the town of Nome, and the only way to get medicine from Anchorage was by dog sled. A half-wolf racer named **Balto** led **Gunnar Kaason**'s sled along the last leg of the life-saving trip.

ARIZONA
THE GRAND CANYON STATE

Arizona is home to many scenic wonders. The mighty Grand Canyon, the Painted Desert, and the Petrified Forest can all be found in this state.

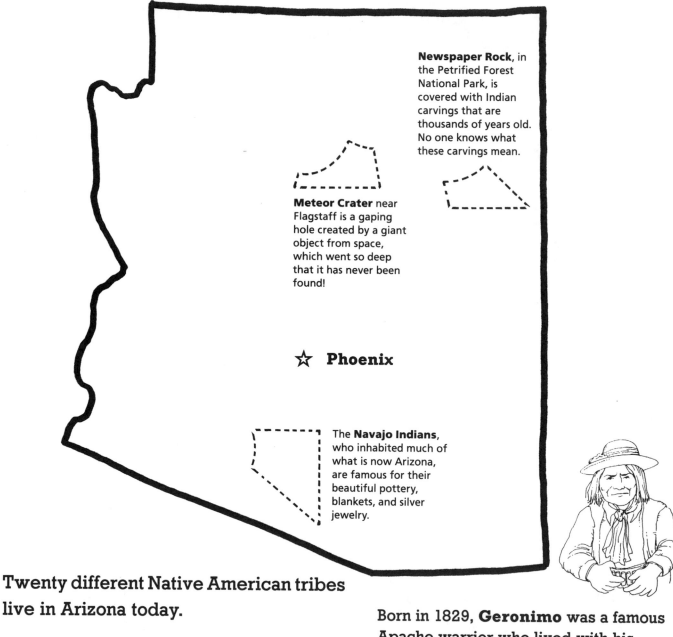

Newspaper Rock, in the Petrified Forest National Park, is covered with Indian carvings that are thousands of years old. No one knows what these carvings mean.

Meteor Crater near Flagstaff is a gaping hole created by a giant object from space, which went so deep that it has never been found!

☆ **Phoenix**

The **Navajo Indians**, who inhabited much of what is now Arizona, are famous for their beautiful pottery, blankets, and silver jewelry.

Twenty different Native American tribes live in Arizona today.

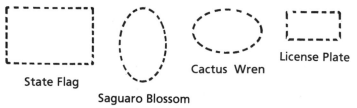

State Flag

Saguaro Blossom

Cactus Wren

License Plate

Born in 1829, **Geronimo** was a famous Apache warrior who lived with his people on the San Carlos reservation in Arizona. Battling for Native American rights, he led many attacks on settlers and soldiers in the southwestern U.S.A. and Mexico.

Find the ARIZONA stickers on sticker page A.

ARKANSAS
THE LAND OF OPPORTUNITY

Arkansas is known for its natural beauty. This state has beautiful caverns, chalk cliffs, forests, mountains, and streams.

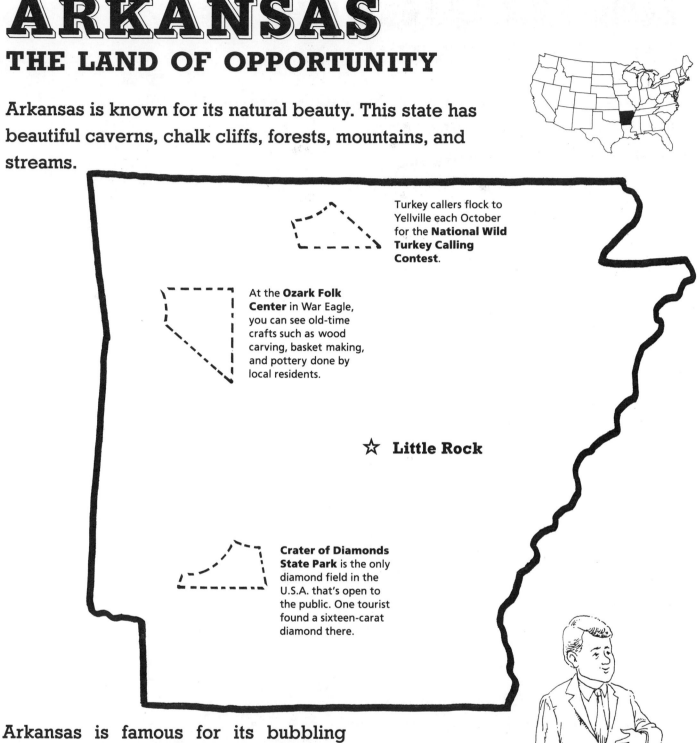

Turkey callers flock to Yellville each October for the **National Wild Turkey Calling Contest**.

At the **Ozark Folk Center** in War Eagle, you can see old-time crafts such as wood carving, basket making, and pottery done by local residents.

☆ **Little Rock**

Crater of Diamonds State Park is the only diamond field in the U.S.A. that's open to the public. One tourist found a sixteen-carat diamond there.

Arkansas is famous for its bubbling spring waters, which are believed to cure body aches and pains.

Born on August 19, 1946, in Hope, Arkansas, **William Jefferson Clinton** was elected governor of his home state four times. In 1992, he won the Presidential election against George Bush to become the forty-second leader of the United States.

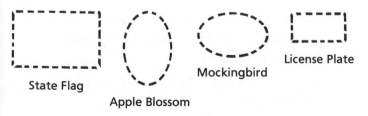

State Flag

Apple Blossom

Mockingbird

License Plate

Find the ARKANSAS stickers on sticker page A.

7

CALIFORNIA
THE GOLDEN STATE

California has it all—tall mountains, sandy beaches, thick redwood forests, and barren deserts.

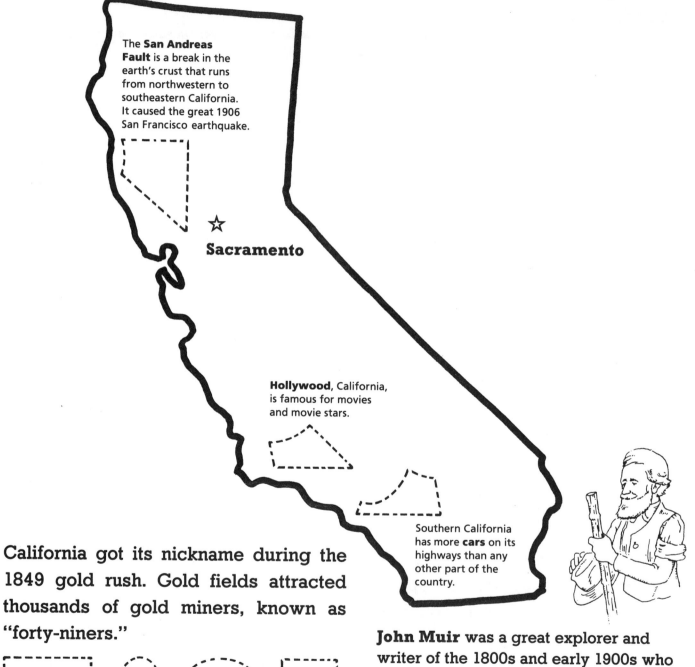

The **San Andreas Fault** is a break in the earth's crust that runs from northwestern to southeastern California. It caused the great 1906 San Francisco earthquake.

☆ **Sacramento**

Hollywood, California, is famous for movies and movie stars.

Southern California has more **cars** on its highways than any other part of the country.

California got its nickname during the 1849 gold rush. Gold fields attracted thousands of gold miners, known as "forty-niners."

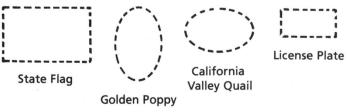

State Flag

Golden Poppy

California Valley Quail

License Plate

John Muir was a great explorer and writer of the 1800s and early 1900s who helped create both Yosemite and Sequoia National Parks. Muir Woods National Monument, one of California's most famous redwood forests, is named after him.

Find the CALIFORNIA stickers on sticker page A.

COLORADO
THE CENTENNIAL STATE

Colorado has fifty-four mountains over fourteen thousand feet high—more than any other state! Amazingly, over one third of the state is prairie land, with no mountains at all!

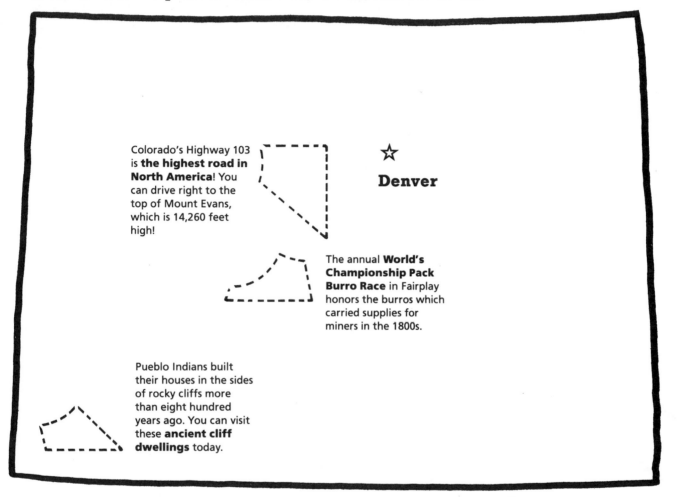

Colorado's Highway 103 is **the highest road in North America**! You can drive right to the top of Mount Evans, which is 14,260 feet high!

☆
Denver

The annual **World's Championship Pack Burro Race** in Fairplay honors the burros which carried supplies for miners in the 1800s.

Pueblo Indians built their houses in the sides of rocky cliffs more than eight hundred years ago. You can visit these **ancient cliff dwellings** today.

The Spanish word *colorado* means colored red. The state was named after the Colorado River, which flows through canyons of red stone.

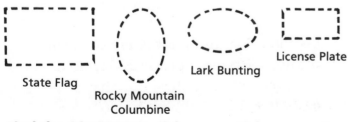

State Flag

Rocky Mountain Columbine

Lark Bunting

License Plate

Find the COLORADO stickers on sticker page A.

Molly Brown is perhaps best known for surviving the 1912 sinking of the *Titanic*. Called the "Unsinkable Molly Brown," this Colorado socialite helped command one of the lifeboats during the famous shipwreck.

CONNECTICUT
THE CONSTITUTION STATE

Connecticut gets its nickname because it was the first colony in the New World to have a written constitution.

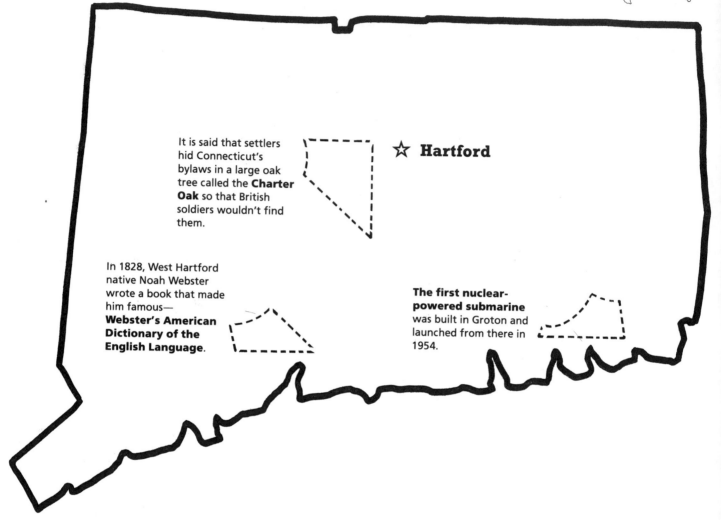

It is said that settlers hid Connecticut's bylaws in a large oak tree called the **Charter Oak** so that British soldiers wouldn't find them.

☆ **Hartford**

In 1828, West Hartford native Noah Webster wrote a book that made him famous— **Webster's American Dictionary of the English Language**.

The first nuclear-powered submarine was built in Groton and launched from there in 1954.

George Washington gave Connecticut a second nickname — the Provision State— because it provided all kinds of supplies for the Colonial Army during the Revolutionary War.

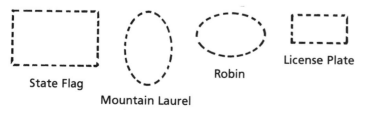

State Flag

Mountain Laurel

Robin

License Plate

Inventor **Samuel Colt** was born in Hartford, Connecticut, in 1835. He created the Colt pistol, the first gun that could fire more than once without being reloaded.

Find the CONNECTICUT stickers on sticker page A.

DELAWARE
THE FIRST STATE

Small but proud, at some points Delaware is only nine miles wide!

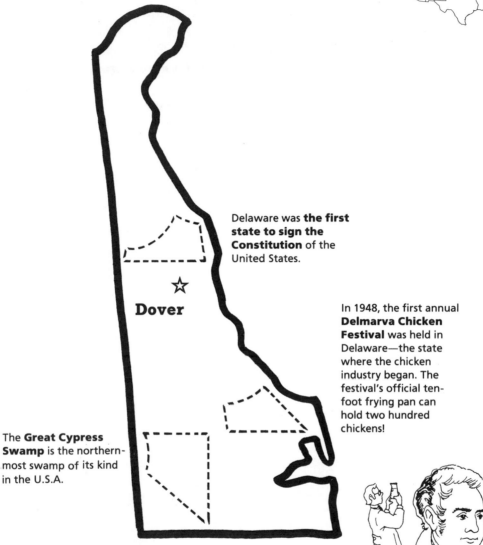

Delaware was **the first state to sign the Constitution** of the United States.

☆
Dover

In 1948, the first annual **Delmarva Chicken Festival** was held in Delaware—the state where the chicken industry began. The festival's official ten-foot frying pan can hold two hundred chickens!

The **Great Cypress Swamp** is the northern-most swamp of its kind in the U.S.A.

One of Delaware's most unique features is Coin Beach, where visitors have found coins they believe washed ashore from a passenger ship that sank off the coast in 1785!

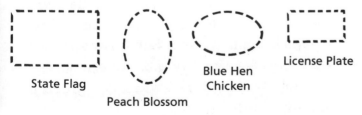

State Flag

Peach Blossom

Blue Hen Chicken

License Plate

In 1802, **Éleuthère Irénée du Pont**, a French immigrant, began a gunpowder company in his new Delaware home. Today, E.I. du Pont de Nemours & Company, with its headquarters in Wilmington, is one of the largest chemical manufacturers in the world and produces thousands of different products—from X-ray film to nylons!

Find the DELAWARE stickers on sticker page A.

FLORIDA
THE SUNSHINE STATE

Florida gets its nickname because it gets lots of sunshine all year long.

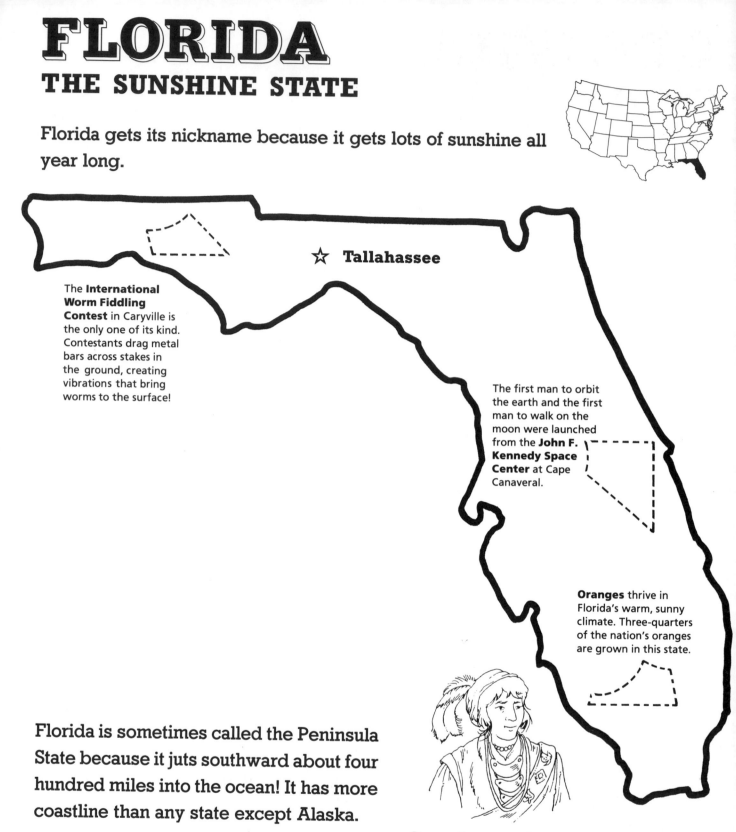

☆ **Tallahassee**

The **International Worm Fiddling Contest** in Caryville is the only one of its kind. Contestants drag metal bars across stakes in the ground, creating vibrations that bring worms to the surface!

The first man to orbit the earth and the first man to walk on the moon were launched from the **John F. Kennedy Space Center** at Cape Canaveral.

Oranges thrive in Florida's warm, sunny climate. Three-quarters of the nation's oranges are grown in this state.

Florida is sometimes called the Peninsula State because it juts southward about four hundred miles into the ocean! It has more coastline than any state except Alaska.

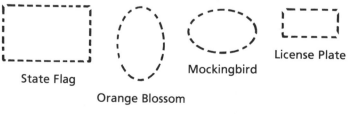

State Flag

Orange Blossom

Mockingbird

License Plate

Osceola was a famous Creek Indian who led the Seminoles of Florida against U.S. troops in battles over Native American land. Betrayed by the U.S. government, Osceola was captured when he agreed to discuss peace.

Find the FLORIDA stickers on sticker page A.

GEORGIA
THE PEACH STATE

Georgia was one of the thirteen original colonies and was named after King George II of England. This state is known for peaches, peanuts, and pecans.

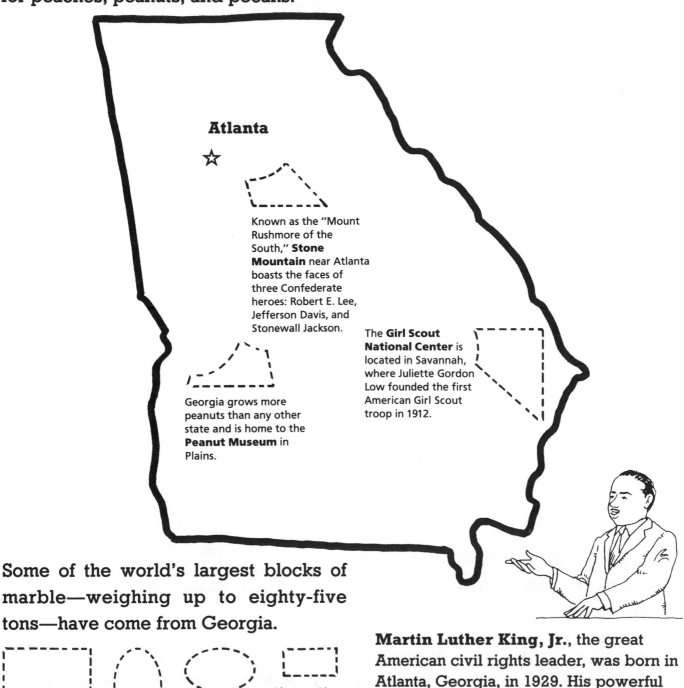

Atlanta
☆

Known as the "Mount Rushmore of the South," **Stone Mountain** near Atlanta boasts the faces of three Confederate heroes: Robert E. Lee, Jefferson Davis, and Stonewall Jackson.

The **Girl Scout National Center** is located in Savannah, where Juliette Gordon Low founded the first American Girl Scout troop in 1912.

Georgia grows more peanuts than any other state and is home to the **Peanut Museum** in Plains.

Some of the world's largest blocks of marble—weighing up to eighty-five tons—have come from Georgia.

State Flag

Cherokee Rose

Brown Thrasher

License Plate

Martin Luther King, Jr., the great American civil rights leader, was born in Atlanta, Georgia, in 1929. His powerful speeches and peaceful demonstrations united people around the world and won him a Nobel Peace Prize in 1964.

Find the GEORGIA stickers on sticker page A.

HAWAII
THE ALOHA STATE

Hawaii, a chain of islands stretching 1,523 miles across the Pacific Ocean, is the only state in the U.S.A. that isn't part of the continent of North America. It's also the youngest state—it was the last to join the Union, in 1959.

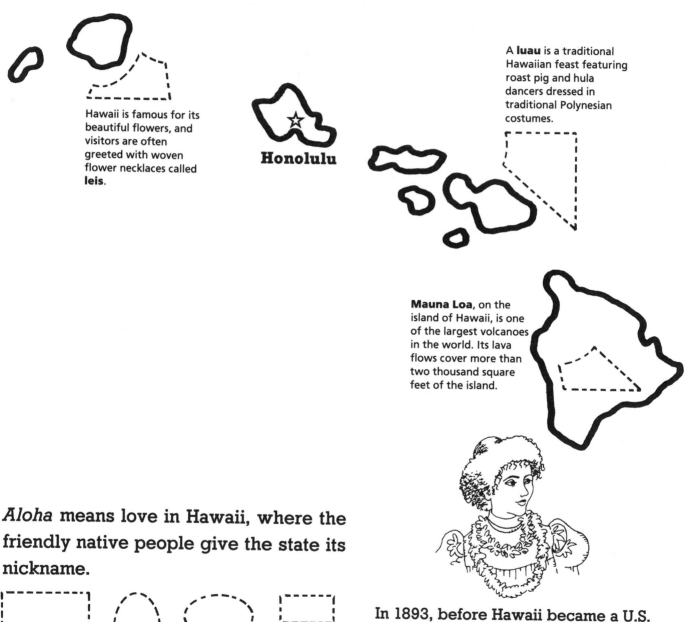

Hawaii is famous for its beautiful flowers, and visitors are often greeted with woven flower necklaces called **leis**.

Honolulu

A **luau** is a traditional Hawaiian feast featuring roast pig and hula dancers dressed in traditional Polynesian costumes.

Mauna Loa, on the island of Hawaii, is one of the largest volcanoes in the world. Its lava flows cover more than two thousand square feet of the island.

Aloha means love in Hawaii, where the friendly native people give the state its nickname.

State Flag

Hibiscus

Nene
(Hawaiian Goose)

License Plate

In 1893, before Hawaii became a U.S. possession, **Princess Ka'iulani** was heir to its throne. Though her efforts to protect her country's freedom failed, the loyal princess was loved by her people.

Find the HAWAII stickers on sticker page A.

14

IDAHO
THE GEM STATE

When the Idaho Territory was established, President Lincoln had a hard time finding a governor who was willing to come to such a rugged place!

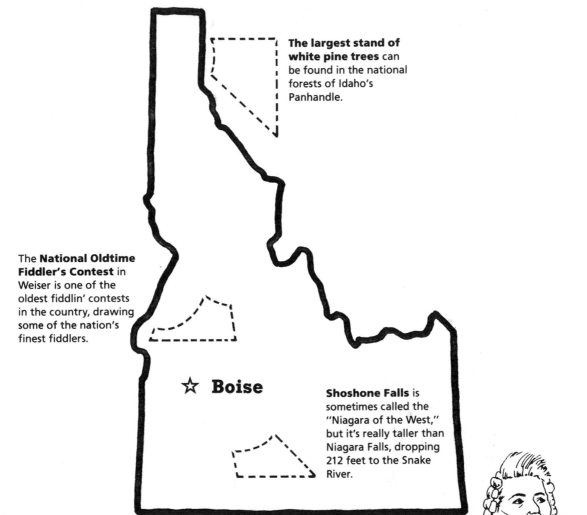

The largest stand of white pine trees can be found in the national forests of Idaho's Panhandle.

The **National Oldtime Fiddler's Contest** in Weiser is one of the oldest fiddlin' contests in the country, drawing some of the nation's finest fiddlers.

☆ **Boise**

Shoshone Falls is sometimes called the "Niagara of the West," but it's really taller than Niagara Falls, dropping 212 feet to the Snake River.

Idaho is called the Gem State because it produces some of the finest quality garnets, opals, sapphires, and rubies in the world.

Chief Joseph was a famous chief of the Nez Perce Indians who lived in Idaho and parts of the Northwest in the 1800s. Fighting for Native American rights, he led his people on a heroic thousand-mile retreat through the Pacific Northwest to Canada.

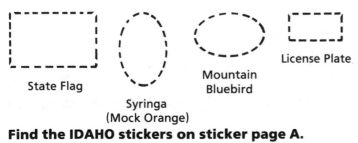

State Flag

Syringa
(Mock Orange)

Mountain
Bluebird

License Plate

Find the IDAHO stickers on sticker page A.

15

ILLINOIS
THE LAND OF LINCOLN

Illinois is understandably proud of its most famous son, Abraham Lincoln, who lived there from the age of twenty-one until he moved to Washington, D.C. as America's sixteenth president.

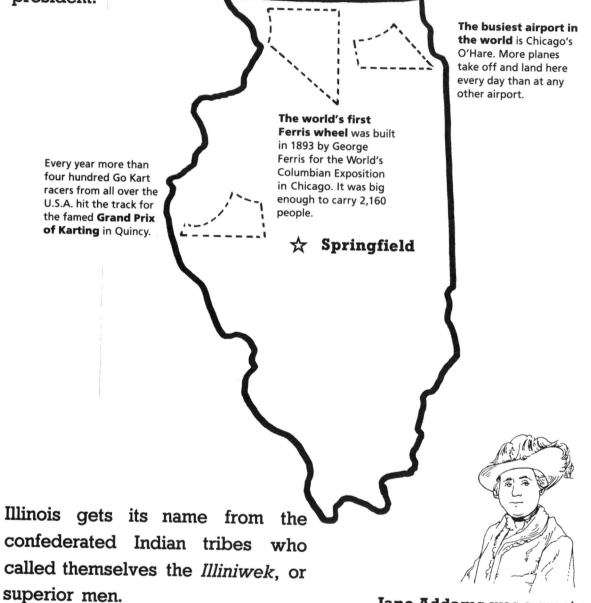

The busiest airport in the world is Chicago's O'Hare. More planes take off and land here every day than at any other airport.

The world's first Ferris wheel was built in 1893 by George Ferris for the World's Columbian Exposition in Chicago. It was big enough to carry 2,160 people.

Every year more than four hundred Go Kart racers from all over the U.S.A. hit the track for the famed **Grand Prix of Karting** in Quincy.

☆ **Springfield**

Illinois gets its name from the confederated Indian tribes who called themselves the *Illiniwek*, or superior men.

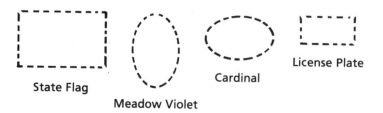

State Flag

Meadow Violet

Cardinal

License Plate

Jane Addams was a great social reformer. Founder of Hull House, a settlement house in Chicago which opened in 1889, she worked for peace and human rights. Born in Illinois, she was honored with a Nobel Peace Prize in 1931.

Find the ILLINOIS stickers on sticker page A.

INDIANA
THE HOOSIER STATE

Indiana is known as the "Crossroads of America" because of its central location. More major American highways intersect Indianapolis than any other city.

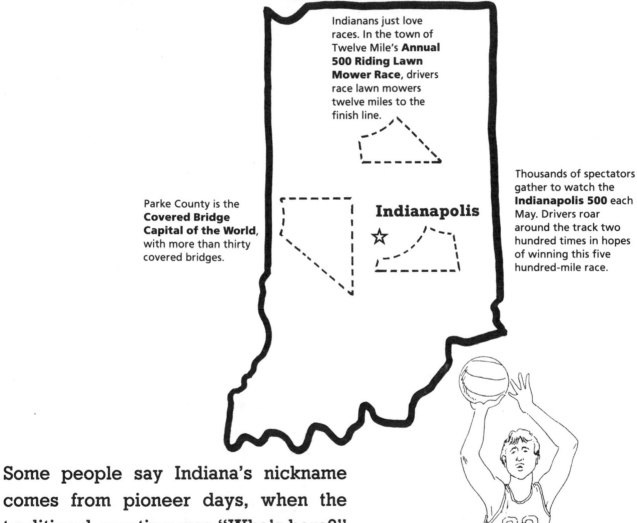

Indianans just love races. In the town of Twelve Mile's **Annual 500 Riding Lawn Mower Race**, drivers race lawn mowers twelve miles to the finish line.

Parke County is the **Covered Bridge Capital of the World**, with more than thirty covered bridges.

Indianapolis
☆

Thousands of spectators gather to watch the **Indianapolis 500** each May. Drivers roar around the track two hundred times in hopes of winning this five hundred-mile race.

Some people say Indiana's nickname comes from pioneer days, when the traditional greeting was "Who's here?" Others give credit to an Indiana contractor in the early 1800s named Samuel Hoosier.

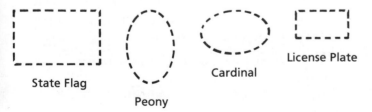

State Flag

Peony

Cardinal

License Plate

Find the INDIANA stickers on sticker page A.

Hailing from the Hoosier state, where hoops are number one, **Larry Bird**'s all-around basketball talent made him one of the best players in the game's history. Born in French Lick in 1956, this superstar led the Boston Celtics to three NBA titles in the 1980s.

17

IOWA
THE HAWKEYE STATE

Iowa raises more hogs than any other place in the world! It's also one of the greatest farming states in the U.S.A., with farms making up about ninety-five percent of its land.

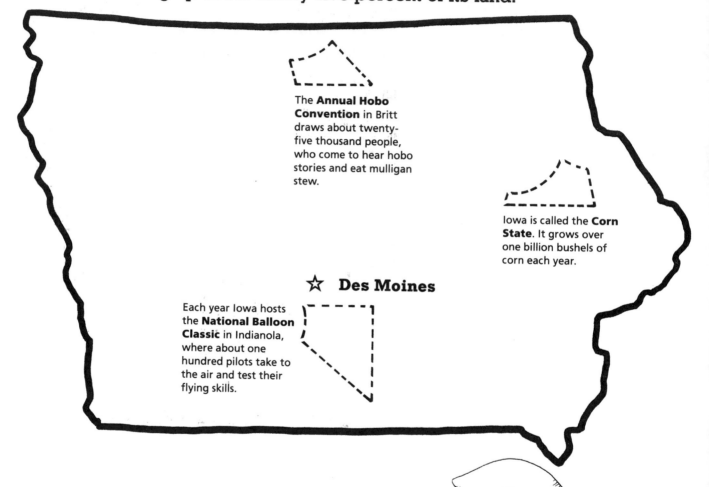

The **Annual Hobo Convention** in Britt draws about twenty-five thousand people, who come to hear hobo stories and eat mulligan stew.

Iowa is called the **Corn State**. It grows over one billion bushels of corn each year.

☆ **Des Moines**

Each year Iowa hosts the **National Balloon Classic** in Indianola, where about one hundred pilots take to the air and test their flying skills.

Iowa gets its nickname from Black Hawk, a famous Indian chief who led a group of Sauk and Fox Indians in the Black Hawk War of 1832.

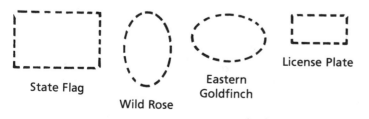

State Flag

Wild Rose

Eastern Goldfinch

License Plate

Find the IOWA stickers on sticker page B.

William F. Cody was born in Scott County, Iowa in 1846. Nicknamed Buffalo Bill because of his expert buffalo hunting skills, he was also famous for his "Wild West" shows—bonanzas featuring cowboy stunts, mock Indian battles, and quick-shooting.

KANSAS
THE SUNFLOWER STATE

Kansas is called the "Breadbasket of America" because it grows more wheat than any other state.

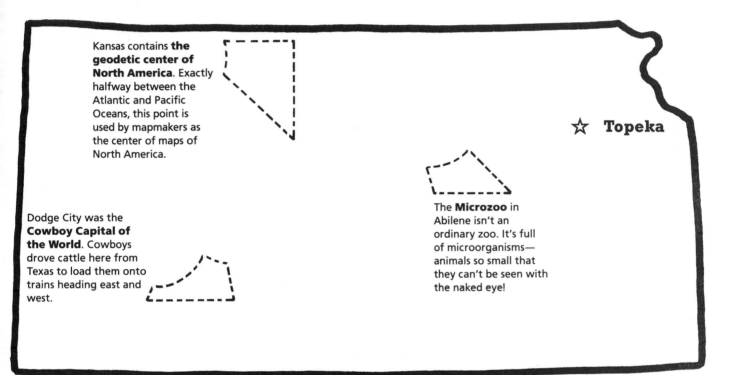

Kansas contains **the geodetic center of North America**. Exactly halfway between the Atlantic and Pacific Oceans, this point is used by mapmakers as the center of maps of North America.

Dodge City was the **Cowboy Capital of the World**. Cowboys drove cattle here from Texas to load them onto trains heading east and west.

☆ **Topeka**

The **Microzoo** in Abilene isn't an ordinary zoo. It's full of microorganisms— animals so small that they can't be seen with the naked eye!

Kansas prairies are often dotted with the bright yellow of sunflowers. These tall prairie flowers are a symbol of the hot, sunny summer days on the plains.

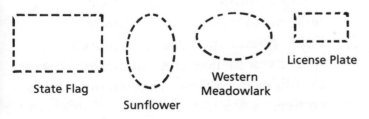

State Flag

Sunflower

Western Meadowlark

License Plate

Find the KANSAS stickers on sticker page B.

Amelia Earhart was a great aviator. Born in Atchison, Kansas in 1897, she became the first woman to cross the Atlantic Ocean by plane and to fly across the Atlantic alone. She made many other historic flights, too, before she disappeared in 1937 on a flight around the world.

KENTUCKY
THE BLUEGRASS STATE

Mammoth Cave National Park in Kentucky has more than 335 miles of winding passageways, making it the largest cave system in the world!

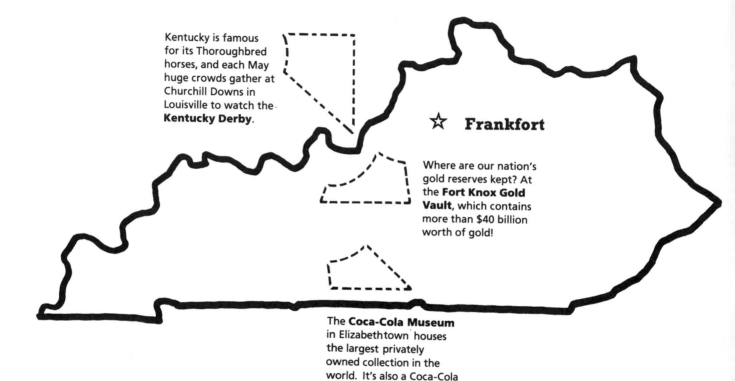

Kentucky is famous for its Thoroughbred horses, and each May huge crowds gather at Churchill Downs in Louisville to watch the **Kentucky Derby**.

☆ **Frankfort**

Where are our nation's gold reserves kept? At the **Fort Knox Gold Vault**, which contains more than $40 billion worth of gold!

The **Coca-Cola Museum** in Elizabethtown houses the largest privately owned collection in the world. It's also a Coca-Cola bottling plant.

Kentucky doesn't really have blue grass. But in the springtime its grasses bloom with dusty blue flowers, making it look blue from a distance.

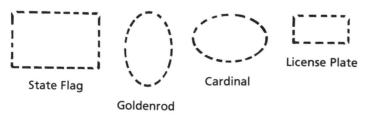

State Flag

Goldenrod

Cardinal

License Plate

Daniel Boone was America's most famous colonial pioneer. Born in Pennsylvania in 1734, he explored the dense woodlands of Kentucky and blazed the Wilderness Road to open the way for settlers.

Find the KENTUCKY stickers on sticker page B.

LOUISIANA
THE PELICAN STATE

Louisiana has an exciting heritage all its own. French Canadians, called Cajuns, who were driven out of Canada by the British settled here. So did French and Spanish settlers from Europe, who make up the Creole culture.

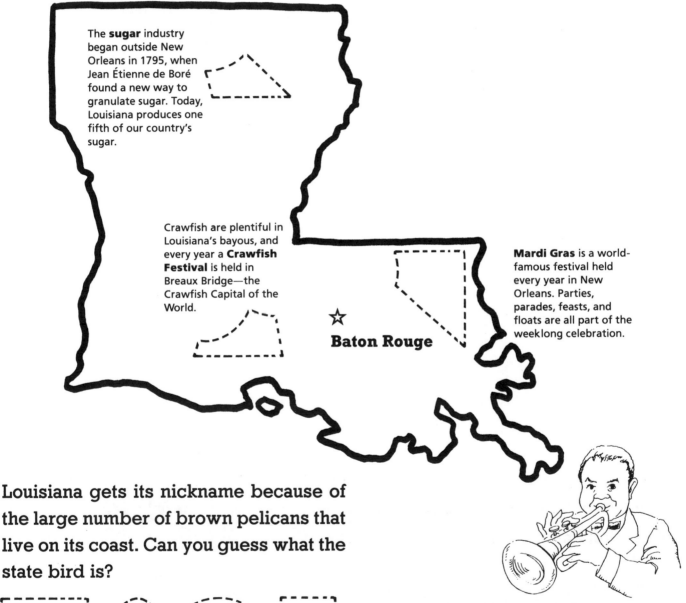

The **sugar** industry began outside New Orleans in 1795, when Jean Étienne de Boré found a new way to granulate sugar. Today, Louisiana produces one fifth of our country's sugar.

Crawfish are plentiful in Louisiana's bayous, and every year a **Crawfish Festival** is held in Breaux Bridge—the Crawfish Capital of the World.

☆ **Baton Rouge**

Mardi Gras is a world-famous festival held every year in New Orleans. Parties, parades, feasts, and floats are all part of the weeklong celebration.

Louisiana gets its nickname because of the large number of brown pelicans that live on its coast. Can you guess what the state bird is?

State Flag

Magnolia

Eastern Brown Pelican

License Plate

Louis Armstrong was born in the heart of New Orleans in 1901. One of the greatest jazz musicians in history, he became famous for his brilliant trumpet playing and unique singing voice.

Find the LOUISIANA stickers on sticker page B.

MAINE
THE PINE TREE STATE

Maine has a beautiful rocky coastline, thousands of offshore islands, and Acadia National Park—the only national park in the Northeast.

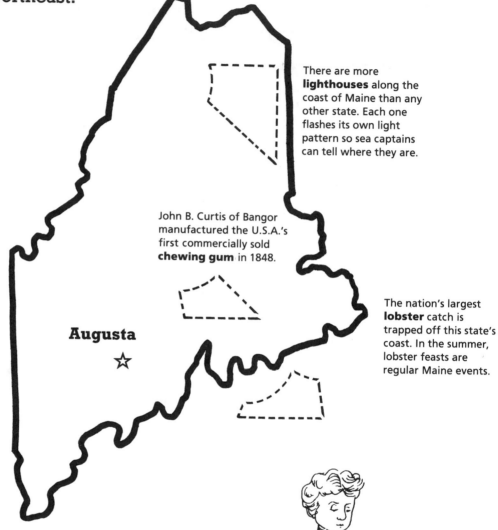

There are more **lighthouses** along the coast of Maine than any other state. Each one flashes its own light pattern so sea captains can tell where they are.

John B. Curtis of Bangor manufactured the U.S.A.'s first commercially sold **chewing gum** in 1848.

Augusta
☆

The nation's largest **lobster** catch is trapped off this state's coast. In the summer, lobster feasts are regular Maine events.

Nearly ninety percent of Maine is covered with pine forests—giving the state its nickname, and even its state flower!

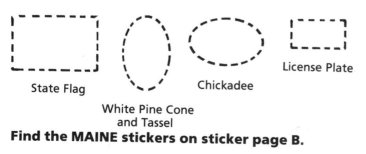

State Flag

White Pine Cone and Tassel

Chickadee

License Plate

Find the MAINE stickers on sticker page B.

Kate Douglas Wiggin, who spent her childhood years in Maine, was an American educator and the author of *Rebecca of Sunnybrook Farm*. Published in 1903, the novel quickly became one of the best-loved children's books of all time.

MARYLAND
THE OLD LINE STATE

Maryland is named for Queen Henrietta Maria, the wife of Charles I of England.

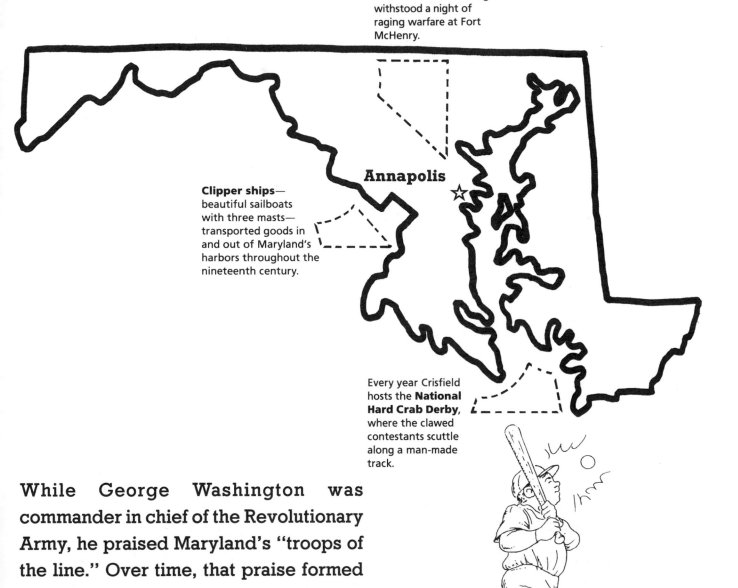

During the War of 1812, Francis Scott Key was inspired to write the **Star Spangled Banner** when the American flag withstood a night of raging warfare at Fort McHenry.

Annapolis

Clipper ships—beautiful sailboats with three masts—transported goods in and out of Maryland's harbors throughout the nineteenth century.

Every year Crisfield hosts the **National Hard Crab Derby**, where the clawed contestants scuttle along a man-made track.

While George Washington was commander in chief of the Revolutionary Army, he praised Maryland's "troops of the line." Over time, that praise formed the state's nickname.

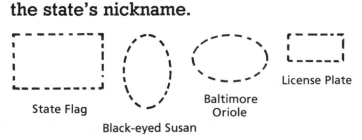

State Flag

Black-eyed Susan

Baltimore Oriole

License Plate

Baseball legend **Babe Ruth** was born in Baltimore in 1895. The first great home run hitter in baseball, he set many major league records and was one of the first five entries into the National Baseball Hall of Fame.

Find the MARYLAND stickers on sticker page B.

MASSACHUSETTS
THE BAY STATE

Massachusetts is first in the printed word. The first newspaper, printing press, and public library in the U.S.A. were all established in this state.

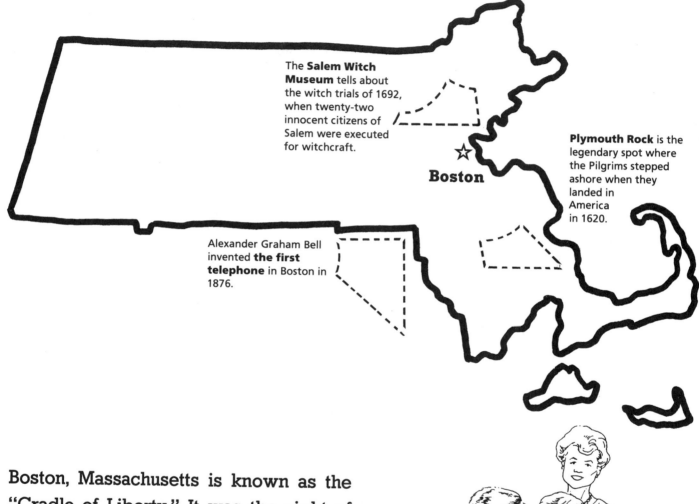

The **Salem Witch Museum** tells about the witch trials of 1692, when twenty-two innocent citizens of Salem were executed for witchcraft.

Plymouth Rock is the legendary spot where the Pilgrims stepped ashore when they landed in America in 1620.

★ **Boston**

Alexander Graham Bell invented **the first telephone** in Boston in 1876.

Boston, Massachusetts is known as the "Cradle of Liberty." It was the sight of major Revolutionary events such as the Boston Massacre, the Boston Tea Party, and the midnight ride of Paul Revere.

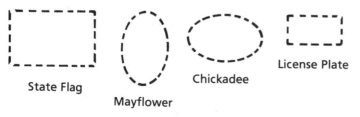

State Flag

Mayflower

Chickadee

License Plate

The **Kennedy family**, famous in American politics, calls the state of Massachusetts its home. Joe and Rose Kennedy had three sons elected to the U.S. Senate, and in 1960, John F. Kennedy became our nation's thirty-fifth president.

Find the MASSACHUSETTS stickers on sticker page B.

MICHIGAN
THE WOLVERINE STATE

Surrounded by four of the five Great Lakes—Erie, Huron, Michigan, and Superior—Michigan has more lake shoreline than any other state!

Michigan's two peninsulas are connected by the **Mackinac Bridge**. Five miles long, this suspension bridge is one of the longest in the world.

Often called **"Motor City,"** Detroit factories manufacture thousands of cars every single day.

☆
Lansing

You can find the **American Museum of Magic** in Marshall, complete with antique magic equipment and personal belongings of famous magicians.

Michigan gets its nickname from trapping days, when French traders brought valuable wolverine pelts to trading posts around the region.

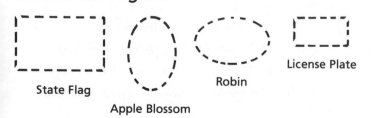

State Flag

Apple Blossom

Robin

License Plate

Pontiac was a famous Ottawa Indian chief who united Native Americans in the Great Lakes region in Pontiac's War in 1763. Pontiac led the lake tribes in a brave but unsuccessful fight against British settlers who had claimed their land.

Find the MICHIGAN stickers on sticker page B.

25

MINNESOTA
THE LAND OF 10,000 LAKES

Minnesota might be called the Land of 10,000 Lakes, but the actual count is closer to 13,000! There are so many lakes that they ran out of names—there are 156 Long Lakes, 122 Rice Lakes, and 83 Bass Lakes in this state!

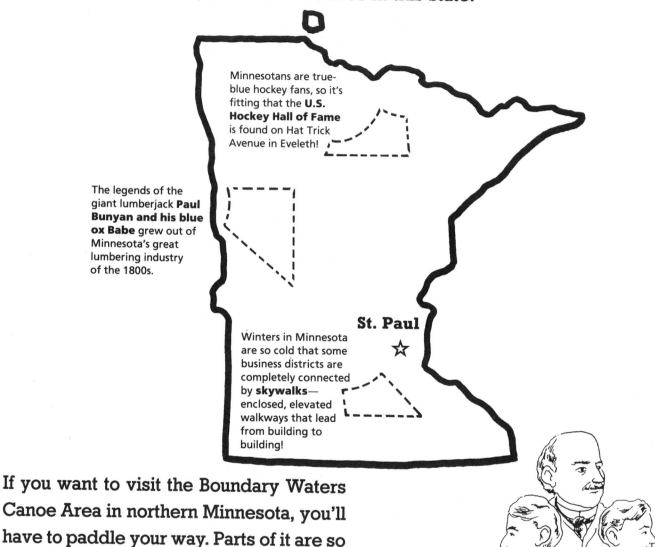

Minnesotans are true-blue hockey fans, so it's fitting that the **U.S. Hockey Hall of Fame** is found on Hat Trick Avenue in Eveleth!

The legends of the giant lumberjack **Paul Bunyan and his blue ox Babe** grew out of Minnesota's great lumbering industry of the 1800s.

Winters in Minnesota are so cold that some business districts are completely connected by **skywalks**—enclosed, elevated walkways that lead from building to building!

St. Paul
☆

If you want to visit the Boundary Waters Canoe Area in northern Minnesota, you'll have to paddle your way. Parts of it are so isolated that nothing has changed there in three hundred years!

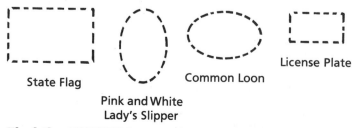

State Flag

Pink and White Lady's Slipper

Common Loon

License Plate

Minnesota is home to the **Mayo clan**, a family of surgeons who founded the Mayo Clinic in Rochester. Started in 1889, this hospital has grown into one of the largest and most famous medical centers in the world.

Find the MINNESOTA stickers on sticker page B.

MISSISSIPPI
THE MAGNOLIA STATE

Mississippi's gardens and forests overflow with lush, beautiful flowers like azaleas and magnolias.

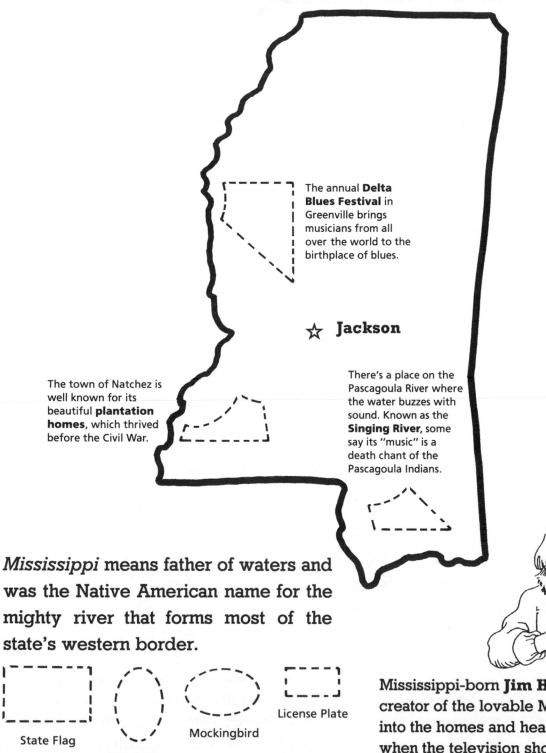

The annual **Delta Blues Festival** in Greenville brings musicians from all over the world to the birthplace of blues.

☆ **Jackson**

The town of Natchez is well known for its beautiful **plantation homes**, which thrived before the Civil War.

There's a place on the Pascagoula River where the water buzzes with sound. Known as the **Singing River**, some say its "music" is a death chant of the Pascagoula Indians.

Mississippi means father of waters and was the Native American name for the mighty river that forms most of the state's western border.

State Flag

Magnolia

Mockingbird

License Plate

Mississippi-born **Jim Henson** was the creator of the lovable Muppets, who came into the homes and hearts of Americans when the television show *Sesame Street* first aired in 1969.

Find the MISSISSIPPI stickers on sticker page B.

MISSOURI
THE SHOW ME STATE

Forty-five thousand caves have been discovered in Missouri. That's more than in any other state in the U.S.A.!

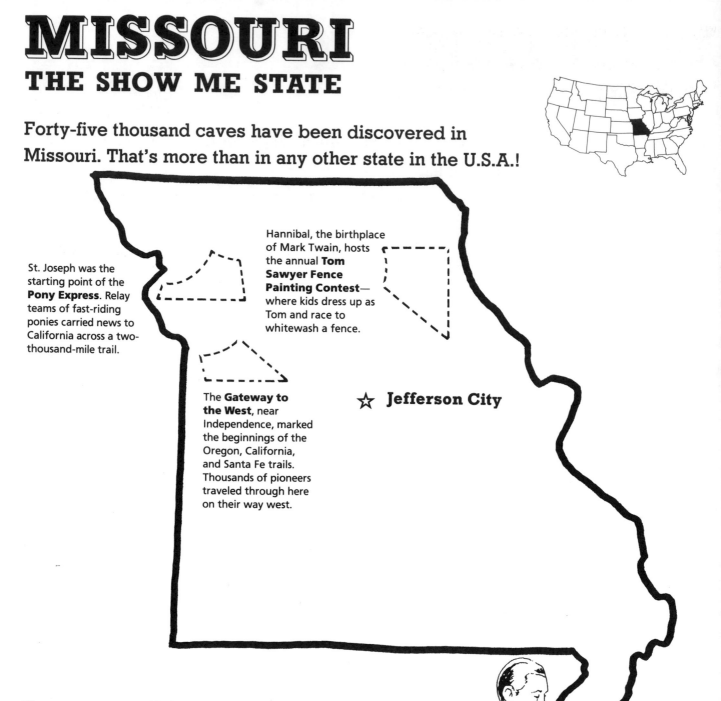

St. Joseph was the starting point of the **Pony Express**. Relay teams of fast-riding ponies carried news to California across a two-thousand-mile trail.

Hannibal, the birthplace of Mark Twain, hosts the annual **Tom Sawyer Fence Painting Contest**— where kids dress up as Tom and race to whitewash a fence.

The **Gateway to the West**, near Independence, marked the beginnings of the Oregon, California, and Santa Fe trails. Thousands of pioneers traveled through here on their way west.

☆ **Jefferson City**

Congressman Willard Vandiver gave Missouri its nickname when he said, "...frothy eloquence neither convinces nor satisfies me. I am from Missouri. You have got to *show me*."

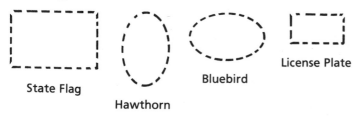

State Flag

Hawthorn

Bluebird

License Plate

Walt Disney is the famous cartoonist who brought hundreds of classic characters—from Mickey Mouse to Bambi—to life in cartoons, films, and theme parks. Much of his childhood was spent in Missouri, on a farm near Marceline.

Find the MISSOURI stickers on sticker page B.

MONTANA
THE TREASURE STATE

Montana's rugged land is home to many animals, including bighorn sheep, grizzly bears, buffalo, moose, and elk.

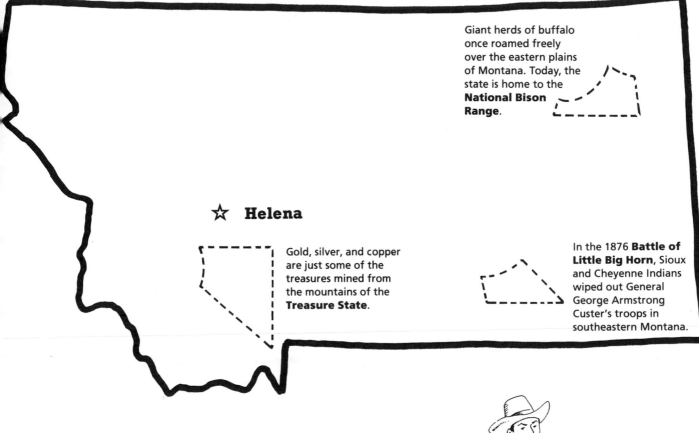

Giant herds of buffalo once roamed freely over the eastern plains of Montana. Today, the state is home to the **National Bison Range**.

☆ **Helena**

Gold, silver, and copper are just some of the treasures mined from the mountains of the **Treasure State**.

In the 1876 **Battle of Little Big Horn**, Sioux and Cheyenne Indians wiped out General George Armstrong Custer's troops in southeastern Montana.

In Spanish, *montana* means mountainous, which is the first thing early travelers thought when they saw the sun shining off the snowy peaks in the western part of the state.

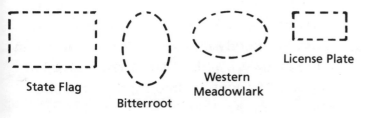

State Flag

Bitterroot

Western Meadowlark

License Plate

Gary Cooper was a famous movie actor known for playing cowboys. Born in Helena, Montana in 1901, he won two Academy Awards and acted in more than ninety movies during his career.

Find the MONTANA stickers on sticker page B.

29

NEBRASKA
THE CORNHUSKER STATE

Nebraska was once called the "Great American Desert." But thanks to the settlers' pioneer spirit, Nebraska has become a center of American agriculture.

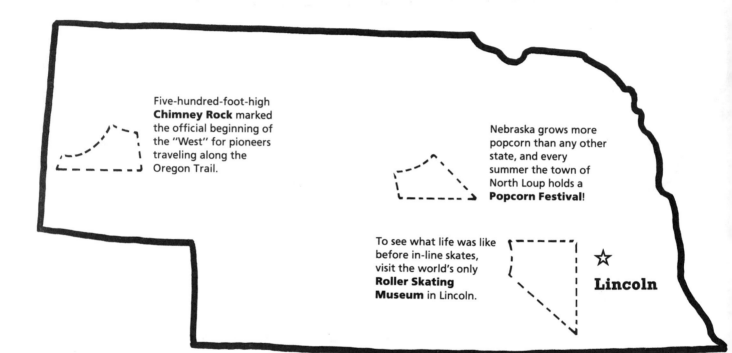

Five-hundred-foot-high **Chimney Rock** marked the official beginning of the "West" for pioneers traveling along the Oregon Trail.

Nebraska grows more popcorn than any other state, and every summer the town of North Loup holds a **Popcorn Festival!**

To see what life was like before in-line skates, visit the world's only **Roller Skating Museum** in Lincoln.

☆ **Lincoln**

Nebraska is the only state with a one-house legislature, instead of the two-house system used by the U.S. Government and the other forty-nine states.

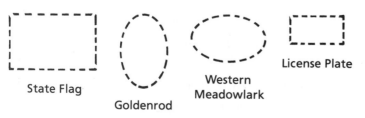

State Flag

Goldenrod

Western Meadowlark

License Plate

Find the NEBRASKA stickers on sticker page B.

Willa Cather was a famous American writer. In 1883, when she was ten years old, her family moved to Nebraska. When she grew up, Willa Cather wrote books about the pioneers and immigrants she met throughout the state.

NEVADA
THE SILVER STATE

The promise of gold and silver brought thousands of prospectors to the hills of Nevada in the 1860s. Today, millions flock to the state looking for fast fortunes in the casinos of Las Vegas.

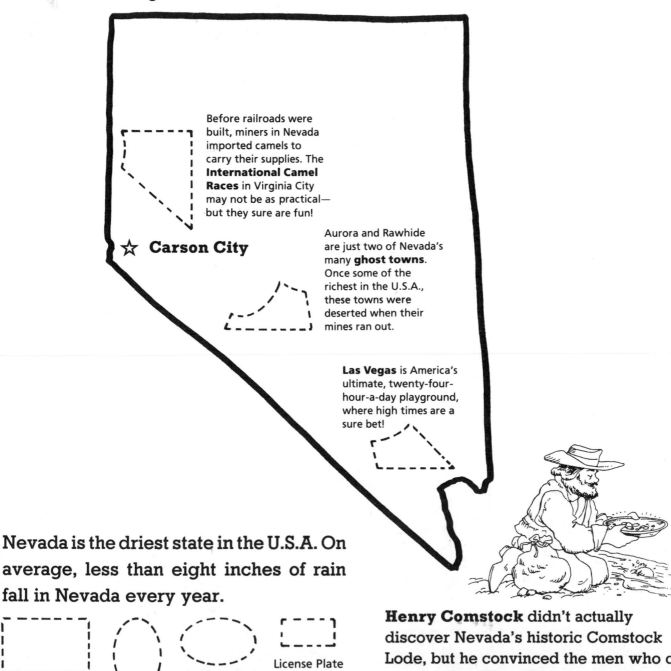

Before railroads were built, miners in Nevada imported camels to carry their supplies. The **International Camel Races** in Virginia City may not be as practical—but they sure are fun!

☆ **Carson City**

Aurora and Rawhide are just two of Nevada's many **ghost towns**. Once some of the richest in the U.S.A., these towns were deserted when their mines ran out.

Las Vegas is America's ultimate, twenty-four-hour-a-day playground, where high times are a sure bet!

Nevada is the driest state in the U.S.A. On average, less than eight inches of rain fall in Nevada every year.

State Flag

Sagebrush

Mountain Bluebird

License Plate

Henry Comstock didn't actually discover Nevada's historic Comstock Lode, but he convinced the men who did to make him their partner. Together they uncovered a vein of gold and silver ore worth $80 million.

Find the NEVADA stickers on sticker page B.

31

NEW HAMPSHIRE
THE GRANITE STATE

New Hampshire was the first of the original thirteen colonies to declare independence from Great Britain, and adopted its own constitution six months before the Declaration of Independence was signed.

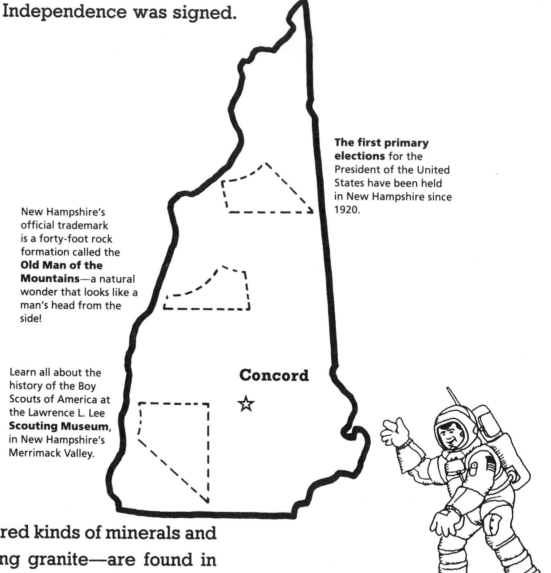

New Hampshire's official trademark is a forty-foot rock formation called the **Old Man of the Mountains**—a natural wonder that looks like a man's head from the side!

The first primary elections for the President of the United States have been held in New Hampshire since 1920.

Learn all about the history of the Boy Scouts of America at the Lawrence L. Lee **Scouting Museum**, in New Hampshire's Merrimack Valley.

Concord
☆

Over two hundred kinds of minerals and rocks—including granite—are found in New Hampshire's White Mountains, giving the state its rugged nickname.

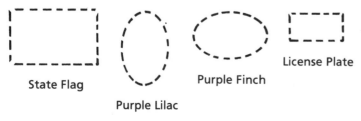

State Flag

Purple Lilac

Purple Finch

License Plate

Alan Shepard was the first American to travel in outer space. He was born in New Hampshire in 1923. His first flight, on May 5, 1961, lasted only fifteen minutes—but Alan Shepard went on to make more trips into space and become the fifth man to walk on the moon.

Find the NEW HAMPSHIRE stickers on sticker page C.

NEW JERSEY
THE GARDEN STATE

Known for its farms and factories, New Jersey also hosts hundreds of beauty contests—from the Miss America Pageant to the Miss Crustacean Hermit Crab Pageant.

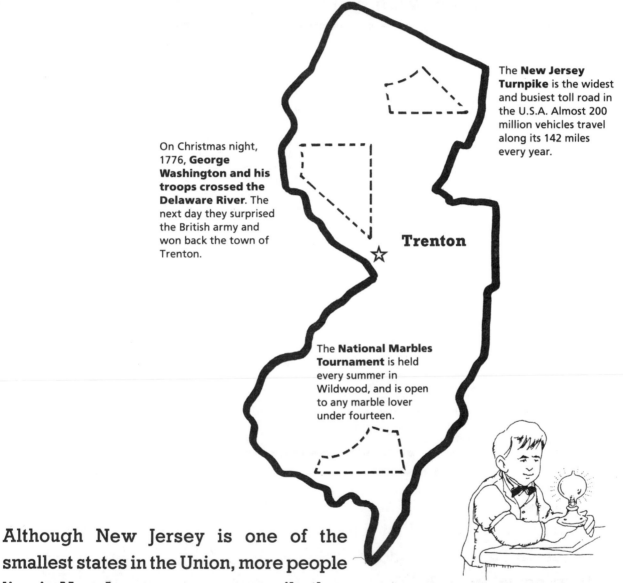

The **New Jersey Turnpike** is the widest and busiest toll road in the U.S.A. Almost 200 million vehicles travel along its 142 miles every year.

On Christmas night, 1776, **George Washington and his troops crossed the Delaware River**. The next day they surprised the British army and won back the town of Trenton.

Trenton

The **National Marbles Tournament** is held every summer in Wildwood, and is open to any marble lover under fourteen.

Although New Jersey is one of the smallest states in the Union, more people live in New Jersey per square mile than in any other state.

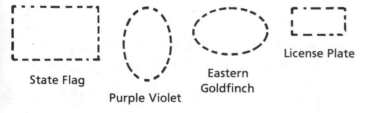

State Flag

Purple Violet

Eastern Goldfinch

License Plate

Thomas Edison's revolutionary inventions were developed in his New Jersey laboratories. The phonograph, electric light, and the movie camera are just a few of more than one thousand inventions Edison patented. Today, his home and labs in West Orange are National Historic Sights.

Find the NEW JERSEY stickers on sticker page C.

NEW MEXICO
THE LAND OF ENCHANTMENT

New Mexico's colorful history dates back long before Columbus! Here you'll find the oldest house in the U.S.A.—an eight-hundred-year-old Indian pueblo—and relics of civilizations over ten thousand years old!

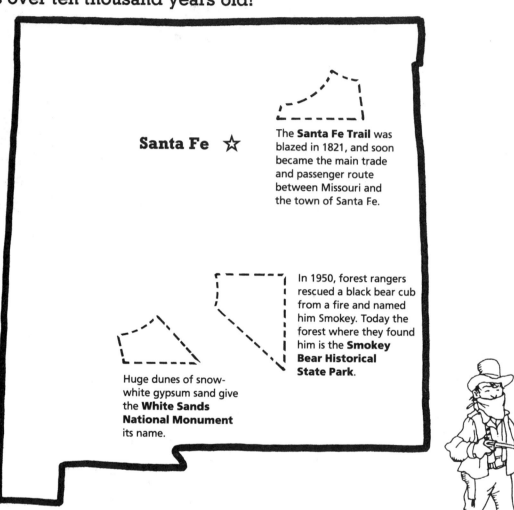

Santa Fe ☆

The **Santa Fe Trail** was blazed in 1821, and soon became the main trade and passenger route between Missouri and the town of Santa Fe.

In 1950, forest rangers rescued a black bear cub from a fire and named him Smokey. Today the forest where they found him is the **Smokey Bear Historical State Park**.

Huge dunes of snow-white gypsum sand give the **White Sands National Monument** its name.

New Mexico's flag bears the ancient sun symbol of the Zuni Indians, but the colors red and yellow come from the flag of Spain, which ruled the area for 250 years.

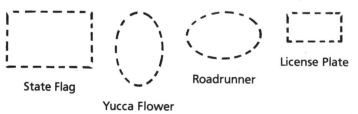

State Flag

Yucca Flower

Roadrunner

License Plate

Find the NEW MEXICO stickers on sticker page C.

Billy the Kid was New Mexico's most notorious outlaw. A good-humored cowhand, Billy found himself on the wrong side of the law when he got mixed up in New Mexico's infamous Lincoln County War. His fearless escape from the Lincoln County Jail is still reenacted there every summer.

NEW YORK
THE EMPIRE STATE

New York isn't only the home of New York City—it's also rich in awesome natural sights like Niagara Falls, the Finger Lakes, and the Adirondack Mountains.

The real **Uncle Sam**, Sam Wilson, is buried in Troy, where he packed meat for the U.S. Army during the War of 1812. The soldiers said that the "U.S." stamped on the meat barrels stood for "Uncle Sam."

The **Erie Canal** was built in 1825 to connect the Hudson River with Lake Erie, and helped make New York City one of the country's major seaports.

Albany ☆

New York City is the biggest city in the U.S.A., with a population over seven million!

Originally called New Netherlands by the Dutch, New York was renamed by the British in honor of their future king, the Duke of York.

State Flag

Rose

Bluebird

License Plate

Find the NEW YORK stickers on sticker page C.

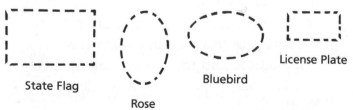

Eleanor Roosevelt was born in New York City, where she later married her distant cousin, Franklin, America's thirty-second president. She became one of the country's most beloved and influential first ladies, and she continued to work for world peace and human rights after her husband's death, as a delegate to the United Nations.

NORTH CAROLINA
THE TARHEEL STATE

North Carolina's Roanoke Island was the site of America's first English colony, but just a few years after it was settled, the colony mysteriously disappeared. Today it is still known as the "Lost Colony."

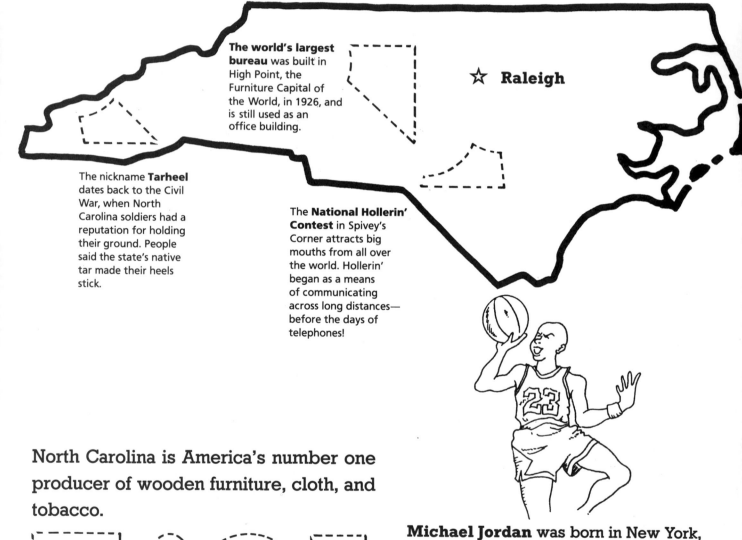

The world's largest bureau was built in High Point, the Furniture Capital of the World, in 1926, and is still used as an office building.

☆ **Raleigh**

The nickname **Tarheel** dates back to the Civil War, when North Carolina soldiers had a reputation for holding their ground. People said the state's native tar made their heels stick.

The **National Hollerin' Contest** in Spivey's Corner attracts big mouths from all over the world. Hollerin' began as a means of communicating across long distances— before the days of telephones!

North Carolina is America's number one producer of wooden furniture, cloth, and tobacco.

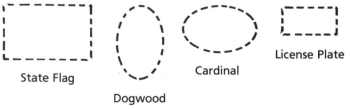

State Flag

Dogwood

Cardinal

License Plate

Michael Jordan was born in New York, but he made a name for himself in North Carolina. He grew up in the town of Wilmington, and rose to basketball stardom playing for the University of North Carolina Tarheels.

Find the NORTH CAROLINA stickers on sticker page C.

NORTH DAKOTA
THE FLICKERTAIL STATE

North Dakota is truly the heartland of America. Not only does the state have some of the country's richest farms and ranches—it also sits smack in the middle of the continent of North America.

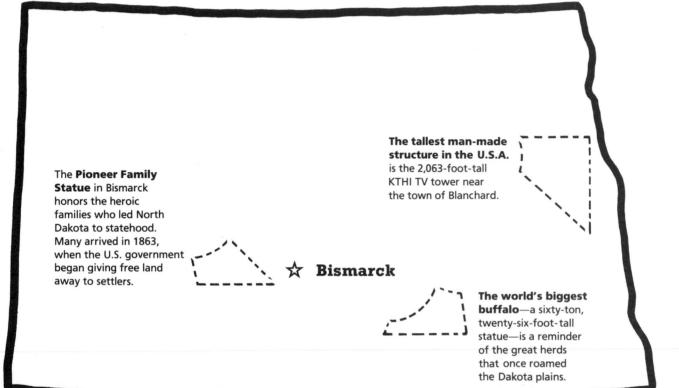

The **Pioneer Family Statue** in Bismarck honors the heroic families who led North Dakota to statehood. Many arrived in 1863, when the U.S. government began giving free land away to settlers.

☆ **Bismarck**

The tallest man-made structure in the U.S.A. is the 2,063-foot-tall KTHI TV tower near the town of Blanchard.

The world's biggest buffalo—a sixty-ton, twenty-six-foot-tall statue—is a reminder of the great herds that once roamed the Dakota plains.

The Dakotas were named after the Sioux, who lived there long before white settlers arrived. They called themselves *Dakota*, or friends.

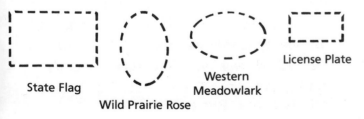

State Flag

Wild Prairie Rose

Western Meadowlark

License Plate

Sacagawea was a Shoshone Indian who traveled as a guide and interpreter for the famous explorers Lewis and Clark. She joined their expedition at Fort Mandan in the winter of 1804, and helped lead them to the Pacific Coast. Without Sacagawea's help, their exploration of the American Northwest would never have succeeded.

Find the NORTH DAKOTA stickers on sticker page C.

OHIO
THE BUCKEYE STATE

The name Ohio comes from the Iroquois word for something great. Ohio was the site of many great American firsts—including the first traffic light and the first Christmas tree.

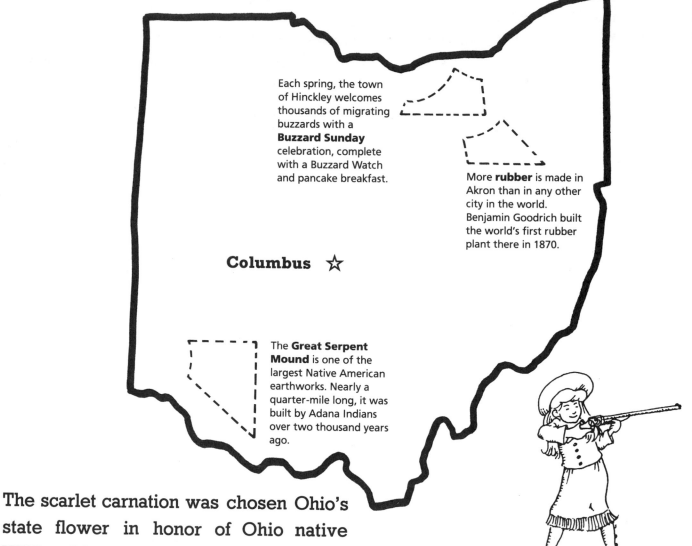

Each spring, the town of Hinckley welcomes thousands of migrating buzzards with a **Buzzard Sunday** celebration, complete with a Buzzard Watch and pancake breakfast.

More **rubber** is made in Akron than in any other city in the world. Benjamin Goodrich built the world's first rubber plant there in 1870.

Columbus ☆

The **Great Serpent Mound** is one of the largest Native American earthworks. Nearly a quarter-mile long, it was built by Adana Indians over two thousand years ago.

The scarlet carnation was chosen Ohio's state flower in honor of Ohio native William McKinley—America's twenty-fifth president—who considered the flower good luck.

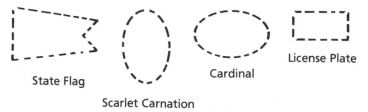

State Flag

Scarlet Carnation

Cardinal

License Plate

Find the OHIO stickers on sticker page C.

Annie Oakley was a famous sharpshooter and the star of Buffalo Bill's famous Wild West Show. She grew up in Ohio, where she learned to shoot before she was eight. By the time she was sixteen, she had turned professional. She was so good, she could shoot a dime from between a person's fingers!

38

OKLAHOMA
THE SOONER STATE

The name Oklahoma comes from two Choctaw words—*okla*, which means people, and *humma*, which means red. Today Oklahoma has one of the largest Native American populations in the U.S.A.

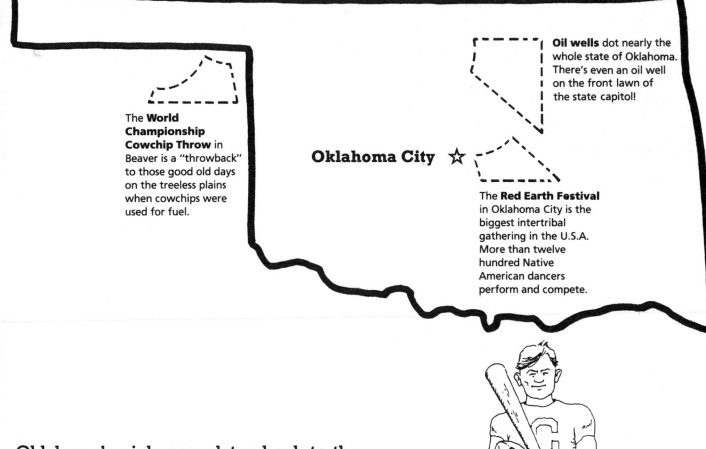

Oklahoma City ☆

Oil wells dot nearly the whole state of Oklahoma. There's even an oil well on the front lawn of the state capitol!

The **World Championship Cowchip Throw** in Beaver is a "throwback" to those good old days on the treeless plains when cowchips were used for fuel.

The **Red Earth Festival** in Oklahoma City is the biggest intertribal gathering in the U.S.A. More than twelve hundred Native American dancers perform and compete.

Oklahoma's nickname dates back to the land rush of 1889, when the government opened land to settlers and some people tried to get the best land by getting there even *sooner*.

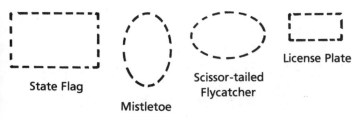

State Flag

Mistletoe

Scissor-tailed Flycatcher

License Plate

Jim Thorpe was born in 1888 in Oklahoma. Called "Bright Path" by his tribe, he has been called the "greatest athlete of all time" by the rest of the world. He is the only person ever to have won Olympic gold medals for both the decathlon and pentathlon. He also played professional football *and* baseball.

Find the OKLAHOMA stickers on sticker page C.

OREGON
THE BEAVER STATE

Oregon was the ultimate destination for thousands of American pioneers—at first seeking fur trade fortunes, and later fertile farmland. Today people still flock to Oregon to see its unique sights and scenery.

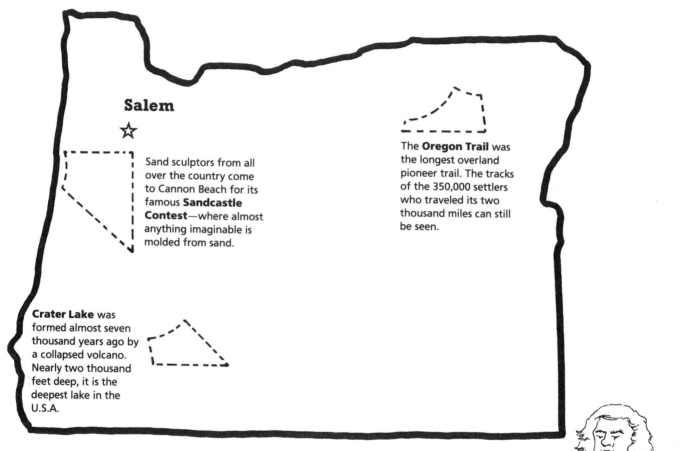

Salem
☆

Sand sculptors from all over the country come to Cannon Beach for its famous **Sandcastle Contest**—where almost anything imaginable is molded from sand.

The **Oregon Trail** was the longest overland pioneer trail. The tracks of the 350,000 settlers who traveled its two thousand miles can still be seen.

Crater Lake was formed almost seven thousand years ago by a collapsed volcano. Nearly two thousand feet deep, it is the deepest lake in the U.S.A.

Oregon is known for being the country's number one lumber producer, as well as for its huge dams along the Columbia River. You can probably imagine how it got its nickname.

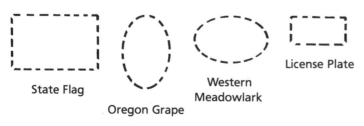

State Flag

Oregon Grape

Western Meadowlark

License Plate

Dr. John McLoughlin is called the "Father of Oregon" because he helped thousands of new settlers make their homes there. Having worked in the area for years for the Hudson Bay Trading Company, he could give settlers advice, good deals on supplies, and medical care.

Find the OREGON stickers on sticker page C.

PENNSYLVANIA
THE KEYSTONE STATE

Pennsylvania's largest city, Philadelphia, served as the nation's capital from 1790 to 1800, and was the site of the signing of the Declaration of Independence *and* the U.S. Constitution.

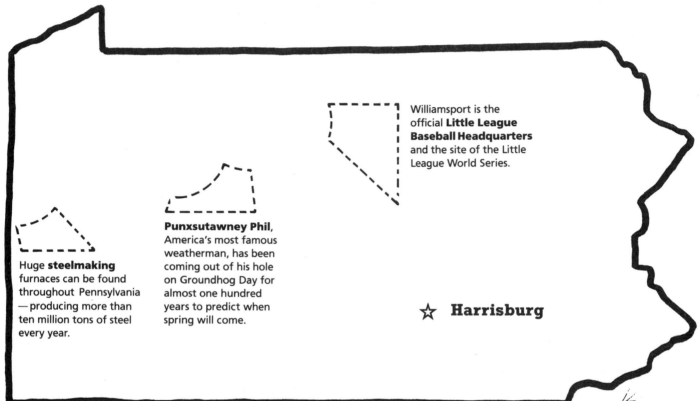

Williamsport is the official **Little League Baseball Headquarters** and the site of the Little League World Series.

Punxsutawney Phil, America's most famous weatherman, has been coming out of his hole on Groundhog Day for almost one hundred years to predict when spring will come.

Huge **steelmaking** furnaces can be found throughout Pennsylvania —producing more than ten million tons of steel every year.

☆ **Harrisburg**

Many Germans came to Pennsylvania in the 1600s and 1700s in search of religious freedom. Today their descendants, known as the Pennsylvania Dutch, carry on many of their customs and crafts.

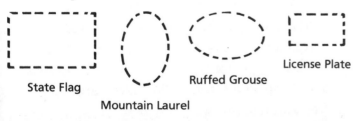

State Flag

Mountain Laurel

Ruffed Grouse

License Plate

Benjamin Franklin was one of America's greatest statesmen, writers, *and* inventors. He was born in Massachusetts in 1706, but ran away to Philadelphia when he was seventeen. There he became the city's postmaster, organized its first fire department, and established the state's first university and public hospital.

Find the PENNSYLVANIA stickers on sticker page C.

41

RHODE ISLAND
THE OCEAN STATE

Rhode Island may be the smallest state, but it's always been big in spirit! Rhode Islanders celebrate their own Independence Day—May 4—the day the colony declared its independence from England!

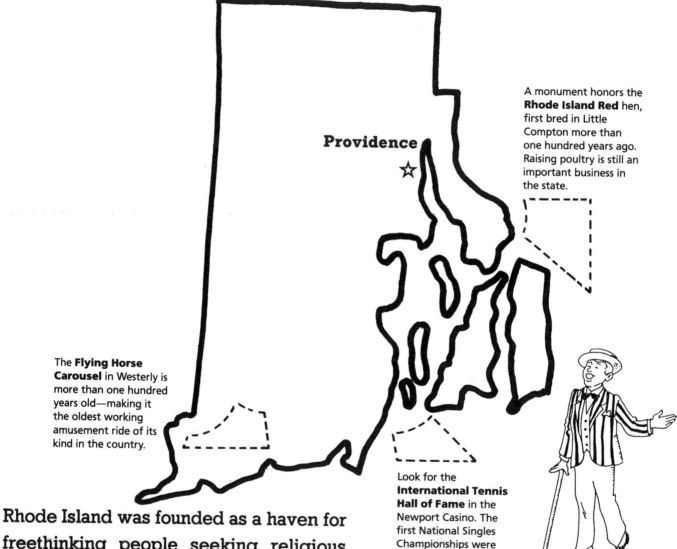

Providence
☆

A monument honors the **Rhode Island Red** hen, first bred in Little Compton more than one hundred years ago. Raising poultry is still an important business in the state.

The **Flying Horse Carousel** in Westerly is more than one hundred years old—making it the oldest working amusement ride of its kind in the country.

Look for the **International Tennis Hall of Fame** in the Newport Casino. The first National Singles Championships were held there in 1881.

Rhode Island was founded as a haven for freethinking people seeking religious and political freedom.

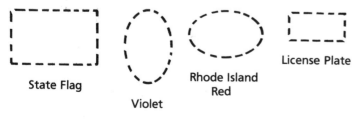

State Flag

Violet

Rhode Island Red

License Plate

George M. Cohan was one of America's greatest popular composers. Born in Providence in 1878, he began writing songs as a teenager. Many of his songs, including "I'm a Yankee Doodle Dandy" and "You're a Grand Old Flag," are still all-American standards.

Find the RHODE ISLAND stickers on sticker page C.

42

SOUTH CAROLINA
THE PALMETTO STATE

South Carolina was the site of 213 battles and skirmishes during the American Revolution—as well as one of the major battlegrounds of the Civil War.

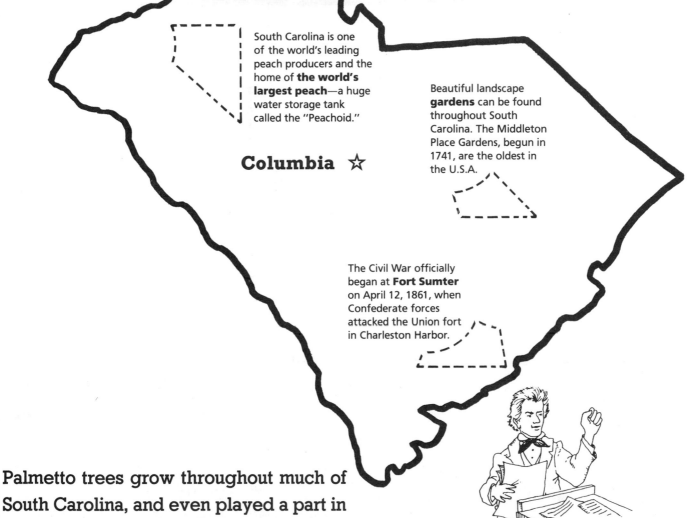

South Carolina is one of the world's leading peach producers and the home of **the world's largest peach**—a huge water storage tank called the "Peachoid."

Columbia ☆

Beautiful landscape **gardens** can be found throughout South Carolina. The Middleton Place Gardens, begun in 1741, are the oldest in the U.S.A.

The Civil War officially began at **Fort Sumter** on April 12, 1861, when Confederate forces attacked the Union fort in Charleston Harbor.

Palmetto trees grow throughout much of South Carolina, and even played a part in defending the state during the Revolutionary War, when forts were built from the sturdy trunks.

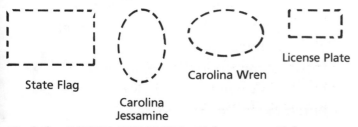

State Flag

Carolina Jessamine

Carolina Wren

License Plate

John C. Calhoun deeply loved his home state of South Carolina. As Vice President, Calhoun sided with his state instead of the nation when he felt taxes were hurting South Carolina's economy. His belief in states' rights later played a large part in South Carolina's secession from the Union in 1860.

Find the SOUTH CAROLINA stickers on sticker page C.

43

SOUTH DAKOTA
THE COYOTE STATE

South Dakota is best known for its colorful and spectacular cliffs and valleys—called the Badlands—as well as for its Wild West history!

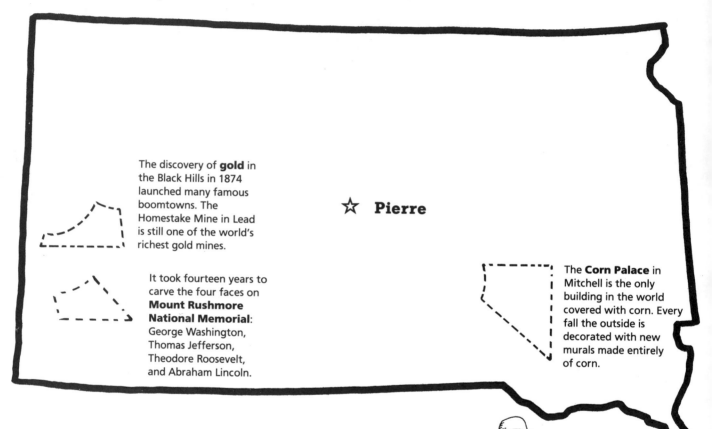

The discovery of **gold** in the Black Hills in 1874 launched many famous boomtowns. The Homestake Mine in Lead is still one of the world's richest gold mines.

☆ **Pierre**

It took fourteen years to carve the four faces on **Mount Rushmore National Memorial**: George Washington, Thomas Jefferson, Theodore Roosevelt, and Abraham Lincoln.

The **Corn Palace** in Mitchell is the only building in the world covered with corn. Every fall the outside is decorated with new murals made entirely of corn.

The coyote is South Dakota's state animal, and lives throughout the state, helping keep down the population of pesky rodents.

State Flag

American Pasqueflower

Ring-necked Pheasant

License Plate

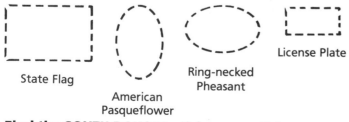

Calamity Jane was a famous frontiers-woman who lived around the time of the great gold rush. She was an expert shot and an excellent rider, but she is most fondly remembered for her heroic care of hundreds of sick people during a smallpox epidemic in Deadwood.

Find the SOUTH DAKOTA stickers on sticker page C.

TENNESSEE
THE VOLUNTEER STATE

From the Great Smoky Mountains to the plains of the Mississippi Delta, Tennessee is famous for its colorful characters and memorable music.

The **Cumberland Gap** is the only natural pass through the Cumberland Mountains and was the main route for settlers coming into Tennessee.

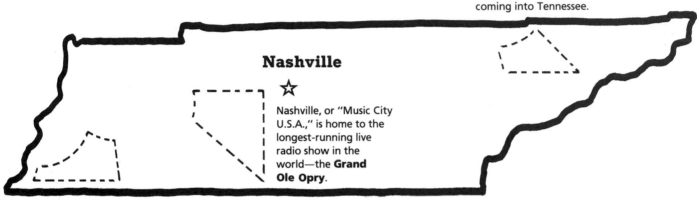

Nashville
☆

Nashville, or "Music City U.S.A.," is home to the longest-running live radio show in the world—the **Grand Ole Opry**.

The **National Civil Rights Museum** is the first of its kind in the U.S.A. It is located in the Lorraine Motel in Memphis, the site of Dr. Martin Luther King Jr.'s assassination in 1968.

One of the best examples of Tennessee's "volunteerism" occurred during the Mexican War. The U.S. Government asked for just three thousand soldiers—but thirty thousand Tennesseeans signed up!

Elvis Presley moved to Memphis with his family when he was thirteen, and began his amazing rock and roll career there six years later. Although Elvis died in 1977, his mansion in Memphis—named Graceland—is still one of the most visited sights in the world.

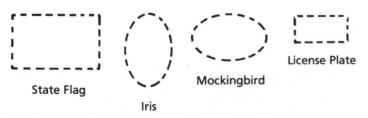

State Flag

Iris

Mockingbird

License Plate

Find the TENNESSEE stickers on sticker page C.

45

TEXAS
THE LONE STAR STATE

It might not surprise you to hear that Texas has more farms and ranches than any other state. But did you know it has over six hundred miles of beaches, too?

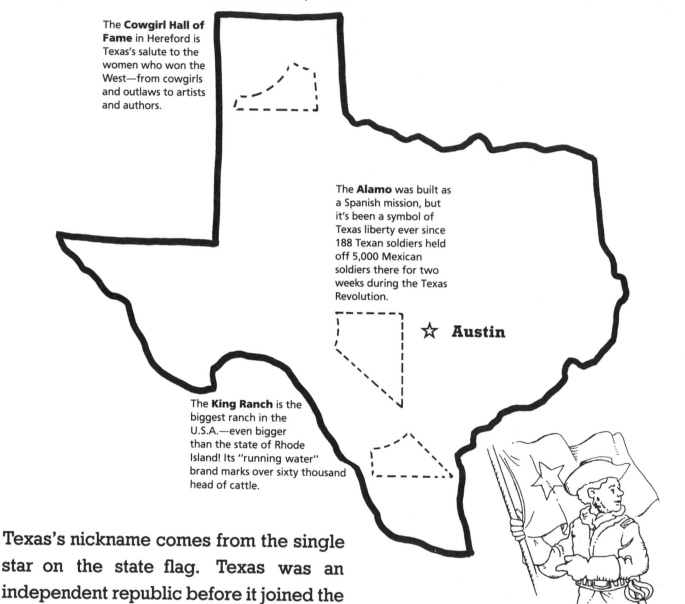

The **Cowgirl Hall of Fame** in Hereford is Texas's salute to the women who won the West—from cowgirls and outlaws to artists and authors.

The **Alamo** was built as a Spanish mission, but it's been a symbol of Texas liberty ever since 188 Texan soldiers held off 5,000 Mexican soldiers there for two weeks during the Texas Revolution.

☆ **Austin**

The **King Ranch** is the biggest ranch in the U.S.A.—even bigger than the state of Rhode Island! Its "running water" brand marks over sixty thousand head of cattle.

Texas's nickname comes from the single star on the state flag. Texas was an independent republic before it joined the Union.

State Flag

Bluebonnet

Mockingbird

License Plate

Find the TEXAS stickers on sticker page D.

Sam Houston was the first president of the Republic of Texas, and served as senator and governor when Texas became a state. He is probably best remembered for his battle cry, "Remember the Alamo!" which rallied Texan revolutionaries to win their independence from Mexico in 1836.

46

UTAH
THE BEEHIVE STATE

Utah's rugged and unusual landscape kept pioneers from settling there until Brigham Young came and decided to turn the wilderness into a home for his Mormon followers.

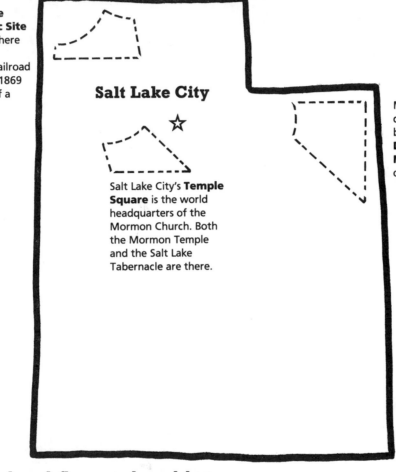

The **Golden Spike National Historic Site** marks the place where the country's first transcontinental railroad was completed in 1869 with the driving of a real gold spike.

Salt Lake City

☆

Salt Lake City's **Temple Square** is the world headquarters of the Mormon Church. Both the Mormon Temple and the Salt Lake Tabernacle are there.

More Jurassic Period dinosaur bones have been found near **Dinosaur National Monument** than in any other place in the world.

Utah's state bird and flower played key roles in its history: Seagulls ate swarms of grasshoppers that could have destroyed the Mormon's first crops; and sego lily bulbs fed people when later crops were lost.

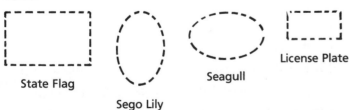

State Flag

Sego Lily

Seagull

License Plate

As the leader of the Mormon Church, **Brigham Young** led sixteen hundred followers from New York across the country in search of religious freedom. When they reached Utah's Great Salt Lake Valley in 1847, Brigham Young declared "This is the place," and that is where they stayed.

Find the UTAH stickers on sticker page D.

VERMONT
THE GREEN MOUNTAIN STATE

Vermont is famous around the world for its great skiing, with nearly five thousand acres of ski trails, and the longest ski season in the country—October to June.

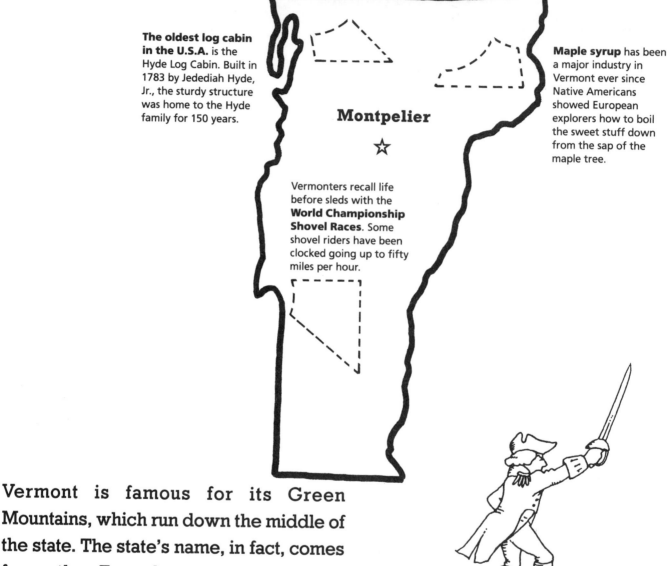

The oldest log cabin in the U.S.A. is the Hyde Log Cabin. Built in 1783 by Jedediah Hyde, Jr., the sturdy structure was home to the Hyde family for 150 years.

Maple syrup has been a major industry in Vermont ever since Native Americans showed European explorers how to boil the sweet stuff down from the sap of the maple tree.

Montpelier
☆

Vermonters recall life before sleds with the **World Championship Shovel Races**. Some shovel riders have been clocked going up to fifty miles per hour.

Vermont is famous for its Green Mountains, which run down the middle of the state. The state's name, in fact, comes from the French words for green mountain—*vert mont*.

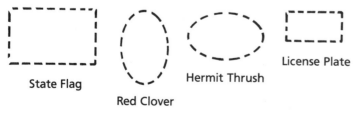

State Flag

Red Clover

Hermit Thrush

License Plate

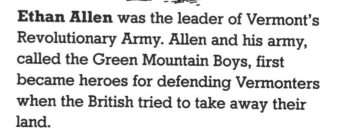

Ethan Allen was the leader of Vermont's Revolutionary Army. Allen and his army, called the Green Mountain Boys, first became heroes for defending Vermonters when the British tried to take away their land.

Find the VERMONT stickers on sticker page D.

VIRGINIA
THE OLD DOMINION

Permanent English settlement of America began in 1607 in Jamestown, Virginia. One hundred and seventy-four years later, American independence was assured when Lord Cornwallis surrendered to George Washington at nearby Yorktown.

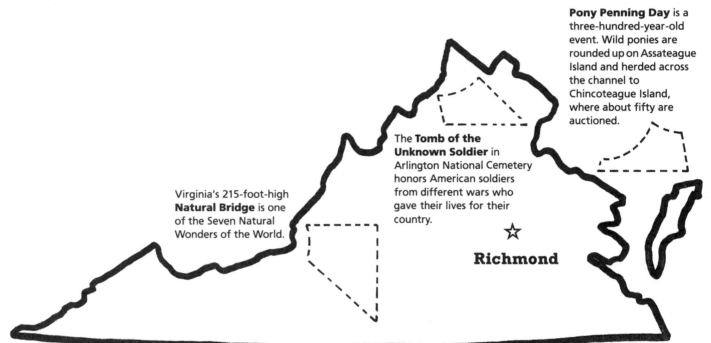

Pony Penning Day is a three-hundred-year-old event. Wild ponies are rounded up on Assateague Island and herded across the channel to Chincoteague Island, where about fifty are auctioned.

The **Tomb of the Unknown Soldier** in Arlington National Cemetery honors American soldiers from different wars who gave their lives for their country.

Virginia's 215-foot-high **Natural Bridge** is one of the Seven Natural Wonders of the World.

☆ **Richmond**

Virginia is sometimes called the "Mother of Presidents" because eight presidents were born there: Washington, Jefferson, Madison, Monroe, Harrison, Tyler, Taylor, and Wilson.

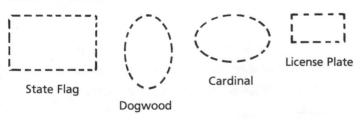

State Flag

Dogwood

Cardinal

License Plate

Thomas Jefferson was not only America's third president, he was also an inventor, scientist, farmer, architect, and the author of the Declaration of Independence. One of Jefferson's proudest achievements, however, was the founding of the University of Virginia.

Find the VIRGINIA stickers on sticker page D.

49

WASHINGTON
THE EVERGREEN STATE

Washington is the nation's leading apple grower, as well as home to breathtaking mountains, forests, deserts, and beaches.

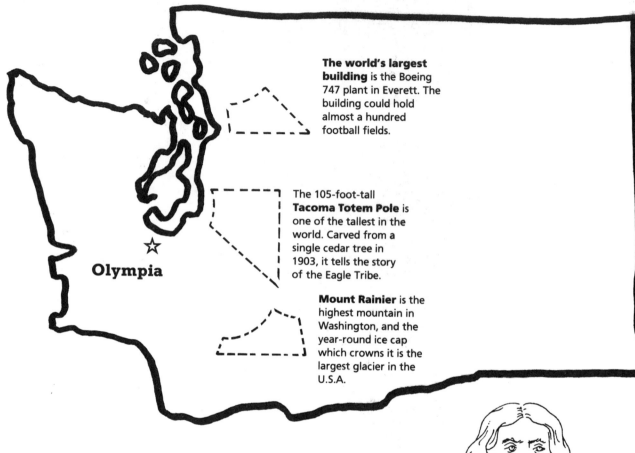

The world's largest building is the Boeing 747 plant in Everett. The building could hold almost a hundred football fields.

The 105-foot-tall **Tacoma Totem Pole** is one of the tallest in the world. Carved from a single cedar tree in 1903, it tells the story of the Eagle Tribe.

Mount Rainier is the highest mountain in Washington, and the year-round ice cap which crowns it is the largest glacier in the U.S.A.

☆ **Olympia**

Chief Sealth was the leader of the Duwamish Nation, which lived in the area that is now Seattle. He was so helpful to white settlers that they wanted to name their town after him. At first Chief Sealth refused, believing it disturbed a person's spirit to say his name after he'd died, but he finally agreed. The name was later changed to Seattle, which was easier to say.

Washington is the only state named for a president!

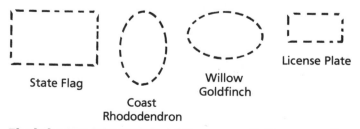

State Flag

Coast Rhododendron

Willow Goldfinch

License Plate

Find the WASHINGTON stickers on sticker page D.

WEST VIRGINIA
THE MOUNTAIN STATE

Hills and mountains cover almost all of West Virginia. There isn't one large area of flat land in the state!

The **International Shrine to Motherhood** in Grafton is where Mother's Day began in 1908. President Wilson later proclaimed the day be observed nationwide.

Charleston
☆

Coal is West Virginia's most important resource. Nearly half the state contains underground coal beds.

The **Green Bank National Radio Astronomy Observatory** has been receiving radio waves from space since 1958. It was the first major radio observatory built in the U.S.A.

West Virginia was part of Virginia until the Civil War, when Virginia seceded and the western counties which now make up West Virginia decided to stay with the Union.

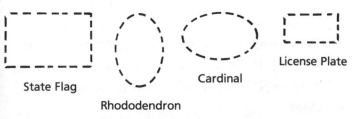

State Flag

Rhododendron

Cardinal

License Plate

Belle Boyd was a Confederate spy during the Civil War. She began spying when she was just seventeen and became an expert in secret codes. Although she was captured many times by the Union Army, her career didn't end until she fell in love with one of her guards and they ran away to be married.

Find the WEST VIRGINIA stickers on sticker page D.

51

WISCONSIN
THE BADGER STATE

Wisconsin makes more cheese and butter than any other state! But its lush forests make lumber and papermaking important industries, too.

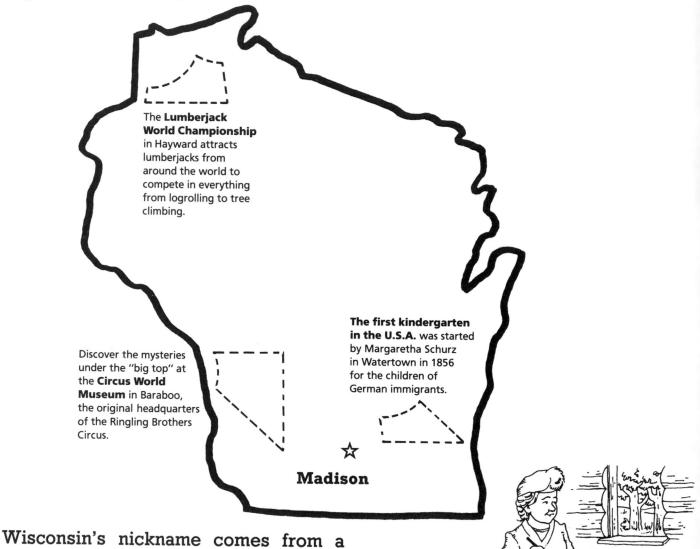

The **Lumberjack World Championship** in Hayward attracts lumberjacks from around the world to compete in everything from logrolling to tree climbing.

The **first kindergarten in the U.S.A.** was started by Margaretha Schurz in Watertown in 1856 for the children of German immigrants.

Discover the mysteries under the "big top" at the **Circus World Museum** in Baraboo, the original headquarters of the Ringling Brothers Circus.

☆ **Madison**

Wisconsin's nickname comes from a name given to lead miners in the early 1800s who lived in caves dug out of the ground—just like badgers!

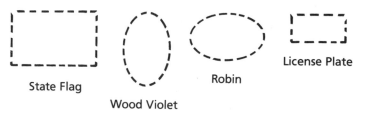

State Flag

Wood Violet

Robin

License Plate

Laura Ingalls Wilder is one of America's most beloved authors. Best known for her *Little House* series, she began her own "little house" days in the big woods of Wisconsin on February 7, 1867. Her family moved to the Kansas prairie when she was only two, but she returned to Wisconsin often.

Find the WISCONSIN stickers on sticker page D.

WYOMING
THE EQUALITY STATE

More than three-quarters of the land in Wyoming is used for grazing cattle and sheep. In fact, these animals outnumber people in the state four to one!

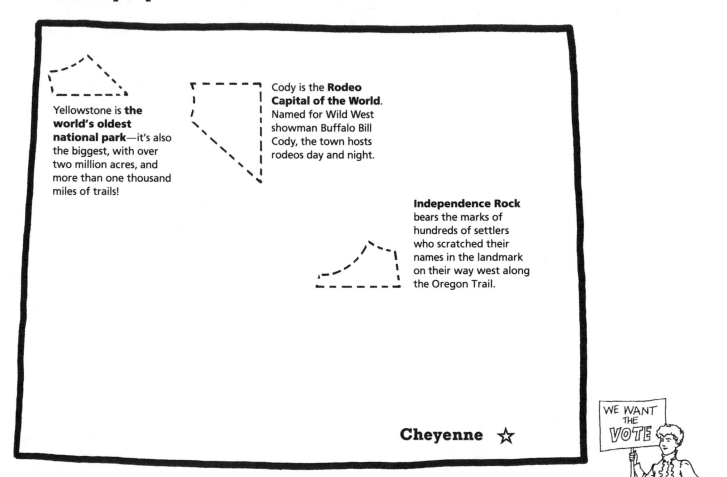

Yellowstone is **the world's oldest national park**—it's also the biggest, with over two million acres, and more than one thousand miles of trails!

Cody is the **Rodeo Capital of the World**. Named for Wild West showman Buffalo Bill Cody, the town hosts rodeos day and night.

Independence Rock bears the marks of hundreds of settlers who scratched their names in the landmark on their way west along the Oregon Trail.

Cheyenne ☆

Wyoming's commitment to women's rights has earned it its nickname. It was the first state to grant women the right to vote and the first to elect a woman governor.

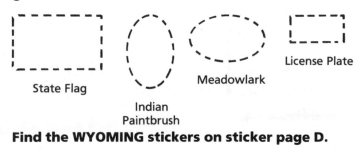

State Flag

Indian Paintbrush

Meadowlark

License Plate

Esther Morris is known as the "Mother of Women's Suffrage." In 1869, she prompted the Wyoming territory to pass the first law giving women the right to vote. She later became the nation's first woman justice of the peace and worked on Wyoming's behalf for a national women's suffrage law.

Find the WYOMING stickers on sticker page D.

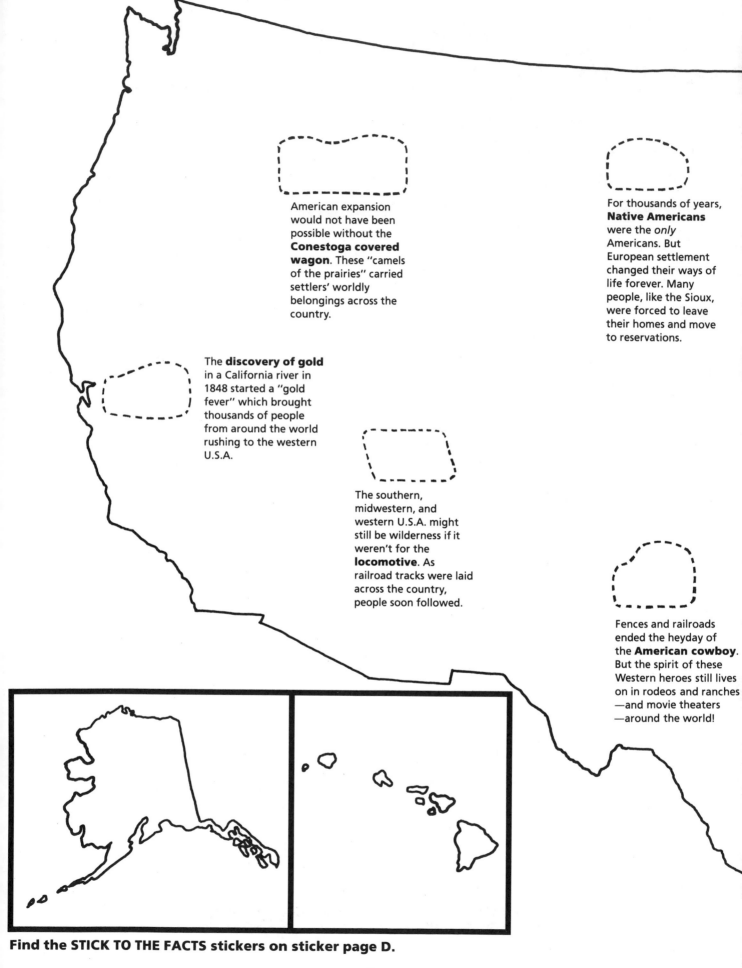

American expansion would not have been possible without the **Conestoga covered wagon**. These "camels of the prairies" carried settlers' worldly belongings across the country.

For thousands of years, **Native Americans** were the *only* Americans. But European settlement changed their ways of life forever. Many people, like the Sioux, were forced to leave their homes and move to reservations.

The **discovery of gold** in a California river in 1848 started a "gold fever" which brought thousands of people from around the world rushing to the western U.S.A.

The southern, midwestern, and western U.S.A. might still be wilderness if it weren't for the **locomotive**. As railroad tracks were laid across the country, people soon followed.

Fences and railroads ended the heyday of the **American cowboy**. But the spirit of these Western heroes still lives on in rodeos and ranches —and movie theaters —around the world!

Find the STICK TO THE FACTS stickers on sticker page D.

The first American Thanksgiving feast was held in 1621 in Plymouth, Massachussetts, when the Pilgrims celebrated a successful harvest with their Native American neighbors.

On July 8, 1776, the **Liberty Bell** was rung in Philadelphia, Pennsylvania, to celebrate the signing of the Declaration of Independence.

Skyscrapers tower over many U.S. cities, but the Sears Tower in Chicago, Illinois, is the world's tallest. It is 110 stories high!

Rising over 305 feet above New York Harbor, the **Statue of Liberty** is America's welcome sign to all the world. It was given to the U.S.A. in 1884 by France as a symbol of freedom for all people.

Henry Ford's **Model T** was the world's first truly affordable automobile. Until Ford began building the car in 1908, only the wealthy could hope to own a "horseless carriage."

The **United States Capitol** in Washington, D.C., is one of the nation's most important buildings. Congress has been meeting there to make America's laws for almost two hundred years.

For over two hundred years, the **"Stars and Stripes"** have represented the U.S.A. The flag's thirteen stripes stand for the original colonies, and the fifty stars stand for the states.

In 1903, brothers Orville and Wilbur Wright made **the world's first airplane flight** near Kitty Hawk, North Carolina, in a plane they built themselves.

From the Confederate Army's attack on Fort Sumter to their surrender at Appomattox, America's **Civil War** divided the nation over the question of slavery for four long, painful years.

Many of America's first settlers lived in **log cabins**. In thickly wooded places where fancy tools were scarce, these simple structures were easy to build.

The U.S.A. landed **the first men on the moon** on July 20, 1969. That day, Apollo II astronauts Edwin Aldrin and Neil Armstrong took "one small step for a man, one giant leap for mankind"!

STICK TO THE FACTS

Mount Saint Helens lost more than a thousand feet from its peak when it erupted on May 18, 1980, leaving behind a huge crater and causing a 250 mile-per-hour avalanche.

About every sixty minutes, **Old Faithful**, the most famous geyser in Yellowstone National Park, shoots a stream of boiling hot water more than a hundred feet in the air.

The **buffalo** is the largest American animal. About 150 years ago, millions of buffalo roamed the midwestern plains. Today there are only about fifteen thousand bison.

Redwood National Park in northern California contains many of the world's tallest trees, including the tallest tree on earth—a 368-foot-tall redwood.

The **Great Salt Lake**, an inland sea in northwestern Utah, is filled with water that's about five times saltier than the ocean!

Death Valley was named by pioneers who were struck by its desolate landscape. The highest temperature ever recorded in the U.S.A.—134 degrees—was recorded here on July 10, 1913.

If you're driving west toward the Colorado Rockies, the first peak you'll see is **Pikes Peak**, which is 14,110 feet high.

The **Grand Canyon** is the largest and most spectacular land gorge in the world. Every year a million people from all over the world flock to this great site.

New Mexico's **Carlsbad Caverns** showcase some of the world's largest and most stunning underground rock formations. Many resemble Chinese temples and frozen waterfalls.

Alaska is the only state where the mighty **grizzly bear** is not a threatened species.

After a rainfall, as the sun's light shines through moisture in the air, it splits into beautiful bands of color forming a **rainbow**.

Find the STICK TO SIGHT-SEEING IN THE U.S.A. stickers on sticker page E.

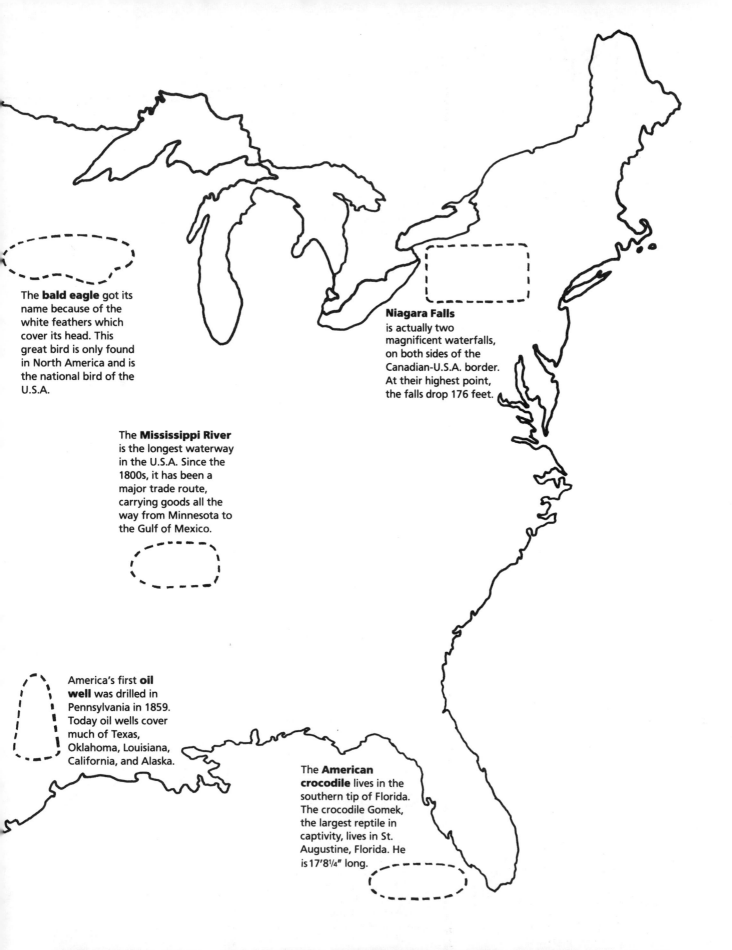

The **bald eagle** got its name because of the white feathers which cover its head. This great bird is only found in North America and is the national bird of the U.S.A.

Niagara Falls is actually two magnificent waterfalls, on both sides of the Canadian-U.S.A. border. At their highest point, the falls drop 176 feet.

The **Mississippi River** is the longest waterway in the U.S.A. Since the 1800s, it has been a major trade route, carrying goods all the way from Minnesota to the Gulf of Mexico.

America's first **oil well** was drilled in Pennsylvania in 1859. Today oil wells cover much of Texas, Oklahoma, Louisiana, California, and Alaska.

The **American crocodile** lives in the southern tip of Florida. The crocodile Gomek, the largest reptile in captivity, lives in St. Augustine, Florida. He is 17'8¼" long.

STICK TO SIGHT-SEEING IN THE U.S.A.

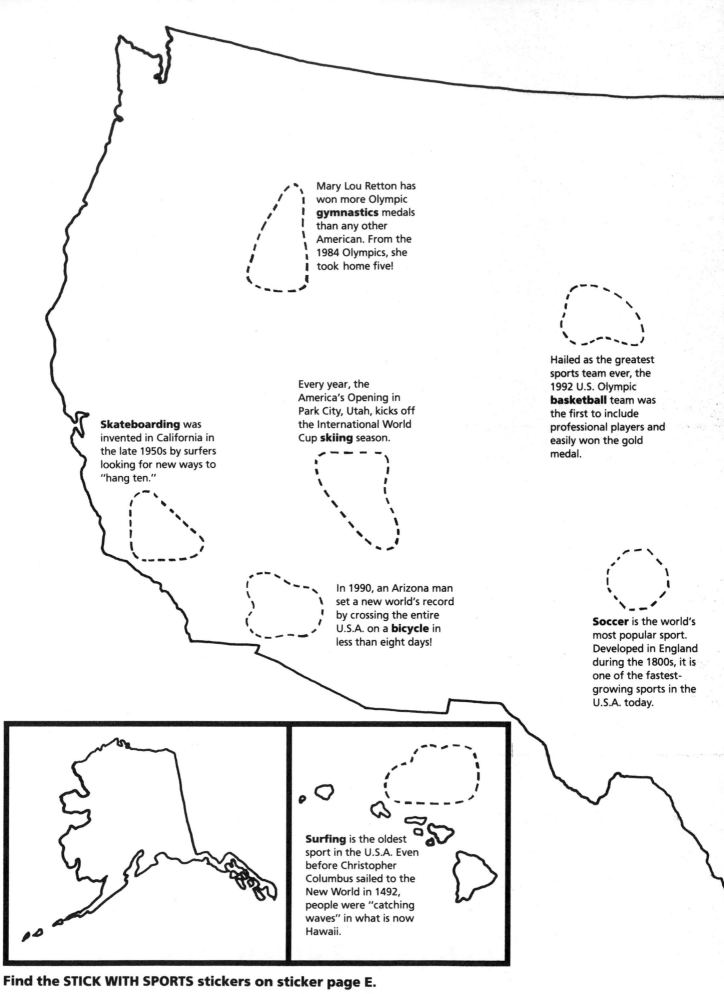

Mary Lou Retton has won more Olympic **gymnastics** medals than any other American. From the 1984 Olympics, she took home five!

Hailed as the greatest sports team ever, the 1992 U.S. Olympic **basketball** team was the first to include professional players and easily won the gold medal.

Every year, the America's Opening in Park City, Utah, kicks off the International World Cup **skiing** season.

Skateboarding was invented in California in the late 1950s by surfers looking for new ways to "hang ten."

In 1990, an Arizona man set a new world's record by crossing the entire U.S.A. on a **bicycle** in less than eight days!

Soccer is the world's most popular sport. Developed in England during the 1800s, it is one of the fastest-growing sports in the U.S.A. today.

Surfing is the oldest sport in the U.S.A. Even before Christopher Columbus sailed to the New World in 1492, people were "catching waves" in what is now Hawaii.

Find the STICK WITH SPORTS stickers on sticker page E.

58

In 1874, Canadian students introduced rugby rules to soccer players at Harvard University and **football** was born.

Basketball was invented in 1891 by a Massachussetts gym teacher. The first basketball players shot soccer balls into peach baskets!

The U.S.A. has won forty-two world championship titles in **figure skating**—more than any other country!

Professional **football** is our nation's most popular sport. The Pro Football Hall of Fame was opened in 1963 in Canton, Ohio.

Legend has it that the first **baseball** diamond was built in a cow pasture in 1839 in Cooperstown, New York, now the site of the Baseball Hall of Fame.

The New York Marathon is the biggest one-day sporting event in the world. Every fall, 2.5 million fans turn out to cheer the twenty-five thousand **runners** through the streets of New York City.

Special Olympics, a world-wide sports program for the physically handicapped, began in 1968 as a day camp in a Maryland backyard.

The first organized **baseball** game was played on June 19, 1846, in Hoboken, New Jersey. The New York Nine beat the New York Knickerbockers— 23–1!

The biggest single **skydiving** formation took place in 1992 over Myrtle Beach, South Carolina. Two hundred skydivers formed five concentric circles, before parachuting to the ground.

STICK WITH SPORTS

Apples are grown in many states, but Washington State grows the most—close to five billion pounds of apples every year.

Idaho produces more **potatoes** than any other state! Baked, boiled, "chipped," or french fried, the potato is America's most widely grown vegetable.

Apple pie was first made in the U.S.A. Although it's usually served as a dessert, generations of American farm families have also enjoyed apple pie for breakfast!

There's a good chance that every **salad** you eat contains at least one thing grown in California—America's "salad bowl." California is the nation's number one farming state.

Lots of popular "American" foods come from other cultures. The **taco** comes from the native people of the Southwest and Mexico, where tortillas are part of nearly every meal.

German immigrants introduced Hamburg Steak to the U.S.A. in the 1800s, but no one is sure who first put the chopped meat patty inside a bun, inventing America's most popular sandwich, the **hamburger!**

Pineapples were brought to Hawaii from Jamaica in the late 1800s. Today they are one of the state's major crops, and one of the country's favorite fruits.

Find the STICK-TO-YOUR-RIBS FOOD FAVORITES stickers on sticker page E.

America loves **maple syrup**. But did you know that it takes around forty gallons of maple sap to make one gallon of syrup?

The world's biggest **cheese** was made in Little Chute, Wisconsin. The wheel of cheddar weighed twenty tons and toured the U.S.A. in its own refrigerated trailer.

According to legend, Native Americans shared **popcorn** with the Pilgrims during the first Thanksgiving in Plymouth, Massachusetts.

The biggest **chocolate** factory in the world is the Hershey Factory in Hershey, Pennsylvania.

More **hot dogs** are eaten in Chicago's O'Hare Airport than at any other place in the world—over two million a year.

No American Thanksgiving would be the same without a **turkey** dinner. In fact, if Benjamin Franklin had had his way, the turkey would be our national bird!

Ice-cream cones were invented at the 1904 St. Louis World's Fair, when a vendor served ice cream in rolled-up waffles—after running out of ice-cream cups!

To celebrate National Peanut Month, a peanut butter company in Atlanta, Georgia, made a **peanut butter and jelly sandwich** that weighed more than seven hundred pounds!

Who wants **pizza**? Thirty thousand people in Havana, Florida, that's who! They all had a slice of one that measured one hundred feet across!

STICK-TO-YOUR-RIBS FOOD FAVORITES

STICK AROUND FOR FUN AND GAMES!

Two or more players or teams can play
these games with the fifty states!

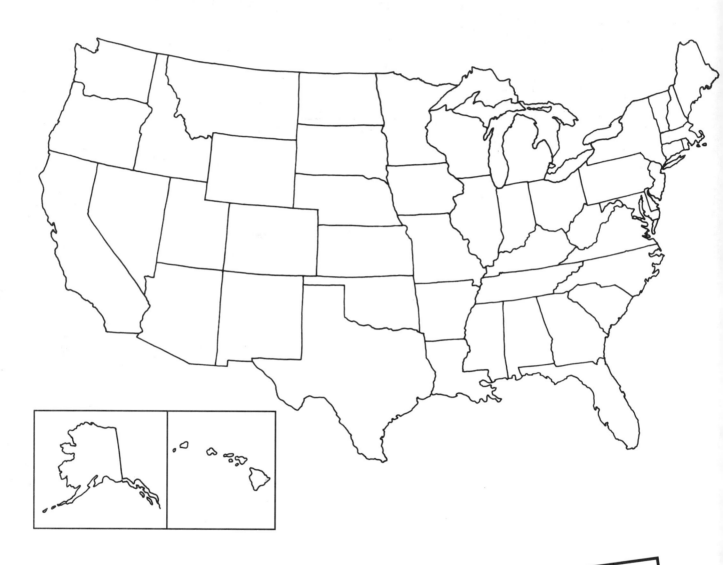

Locate the State

One player names a state, and the next player has to find it on the map. Each player has ten seconds. When a player can't locate the state, he or she is out of the game. The last player in the game is the winner.

Another way to play: one player points to a state on the map and the other player tries to name it.

Way to Go

What states would you travel through if you were taking a trip from Montana to Oklahoma? Find a way that takes you through the fewest states.

Next find a way to go from Washington to Florida. Try to travel through as few states as possible.

Map out a trip from Maine to California. Can you name all the states you'll go through?

Over the Border

One player calls out a state, and the next player must name a state that's beside it. Players who can't name a border state are out of the game, and the last player in the game is the winner.

Capital Combat

In this game, one player calls out a state, and the next player has to name that state's capital. Players who miss the capital city are out, and the last player in the game wins.

You can also try playing a round backwards, with one player calling out a capital city and the next player naming the state.

String of States

The first player in this game calls out the name of a state: Missouri, for instance. The second player has to name a state that begins with the last letter in the first state's name: "i" in this case. So the second player might say Idaho. Then the next player must name a state that begins with the last letter in Idaho. Each state may be used only once. When a player is stumped, he or she is out of the game. The last player in the game wins.

License Plate Travel Games

Whether you're traveling cross-country or just across town, you can have fun in the car playing these games that use automobile license plates from the fifty states!

Spot the Secret Numbers

One player thinks of two numbers or two letters for the next player to find on a license plate. If he spots one of those numbers or letters, he gets 50 points. If he spots both numbers or letters on the same plate, he gets 100 points. The first player to collect 500 points wins.

Add 'em Up!

In this game, players take turns spotting a license plate and adding up the numbers on it. For instance, 2 3 7 - A B C on a license plate would be 2 + 3 + 7 = 12 points. (Letters are not worth any points.) The first player to get 50 points wins.

Your State Plate Collection

Keep a record of all the different license plates you see. Mark down when and where you spotted each plate. How many states are in your collection?

10—**FAIR.** A good beginning!
15—**GOOD.** Keep collecting!
25—**VERY GOOD.** Half the U.S.A.!
30—**OUTSTANDING.**
  A dedicated collector!
40—**EXCELLENT.**
  Amaze your friends!
50—**SUPERLATIVE.**
  A rare collection!

Alphabet Hunt

In this game, players try to find all the letters of the alphabet on license plates. The letters must be found in order, beginning with A. Players can't save letters and use them later. Players can collect only one letter per license plate. The winner is the first one to get to Z or the player with the most letters at the end of twenty minutes.

So that both teams can play at the same time, one player should sit on the left side of the car and the other should sit on the right. Players switch sides halfway through the game.

Traveling H-O-R-S-E

Have you ever noticed that the letters on some license plates almost make words? For example, F S H almost makes "fish." H D G looks almost like "hot dog." G S T could be "ghost."

In this game, players spot license plate letters and try to make words out of them. If a player is stumped and can't make a word, she collects one letter in the word HORSE. When a player gets H-O-R-S-E, she's out of the game. The last player in the game is the winner. Now you can horse around in the backseat all you want!